I0672439

Liido
Beach

AFDHERE JAMA

Copyright © 2018 by the Author.

All rights reserved.

ISBN: 0-9800138-0-1
ISBN-13: 978-0-9800138-0-1

DEDICATION

To story lovers everywhere.

CONTENTS

PROLOGUE

Somewhere out of the billions of the planets in this galaxy, an energy forms and heads to Earth. The intelligent energy zooms in on the globe until the African continent is in its view. Further zooming brings the energy to Mogadishu. Now we are in the Howlwadaag part of town. There is a colorful little villa on Muuse Galaal Street, just halfway between Muuse Galaal Secondary School and Ahmed Gurey Primary School. Inside, in the second room from the left, the energy observes from the clock on the wall that it is just a little after seven in the morning.

Hanad, the most handsome young man this energy had ever seen, is sleeping in his bed. He is sleeping carelessly, as part of his body—one arm and a leg—are on the floor. There is a hint of a smile on his face, and if one listens carefully one can hear the seventeen-year-old is snoring lightly.

Hanad is in the middle of a dream.

In the dream, the young man is in a massive desert. He is sitting under a huge *qurac*, an acacia tree, which is the only tree one could find as far as the eye can see. He is waiting for his lover.

At the same time, as the young man wonders where his lover is, the energy enters the dream.

The energy turns into a being composed of golden pieces of fire. The being turns into a human-looking male. The man is a *jinn*, a demon.

"Finally," complains the demon.

He stands in front of Hanad, although the young man cannot see him, and looks into the face. The demon is looking for someone, but he is unsure whether the person he's looking for is Hanad. He needs to get the young man to stand up, so the demon starts looking around. It is as though he is looking for something to get Hanad's attention.

"Shit," says the demon.

He doesn't find anything. Instead, the demon blows towards Hanad, which makes the young man feel a bit of a chill on his face and leads him to stand up.

"Hhhmmm," smiles the demon.

To the demon, Hanad looks like a typical Somali. He observes that the young man is tall and slim in size. He focuses momentarily on Hanad's drawn-out forehead, and stays longer on the aquiline nose, as it reminds the demon of the curved beak of an eagle he once kept as a pet. The full lips of the young man, which parted somewhere in Hanad's wandering thoughts, make the demon stare even longer.

Good thing he can't see me, thinks the demon.

The demon realizes it is not the young man he was looking for, although one can see for a moment he thinks it was the same young man.

"Hhhmm," he says, unsure.

To make sure, the demon gets closer and looks into Hanad's eyes. He shakes his head and goes deeper. Deeper. Deeper.

"Oh," he steps back, shocked. He is shaken by what he saw. He saw that Hanad is probably the purest human he had ever seen. Not even a shred of evil could he find in him.

"Fucking humans," groans the demon.

Just like that, the disappointed demon leaves as fast as he had appeared.

Hanad wakes up from his dream.

CHAPTER 1

Somewhere out of the billions of the planets in this galaxy, an energy forms and heads to Earth. The intelligent energy zooms in on the globe until the African continent is in its view.

"Welcome to Mogadishu." says the Somali Airlines flight attendant over the speakers, "It is eighty-two degrees and sunny," she adds, sounding as if she is reading all of this from material she hasn't had time to practice with.

Farah looks around, watching with shock all of these eager Somali travelers that are already standing up in the aisles and opening the overhead compartments, as the plane makes its way on the tarmac. More importantly, he is a bit taken aback by the fact that the hostesses don't stop them.

"Thank you, Allah," says his mother, sitting next to him, interrupting her son's staring into faces judgmentally.

Farah shakes his head and turns to his mother. He momentarily forgot that she hates to fly, and especially hates takeoffs and landings.

"Are you alright?" Farah asks.

"Yes," she says, relieved. "I'm fine."

Mogadishu's International Airport is in much better shape than Farah had imagined. It is bigger and cleaner. Despite the chaotic passengers he and his mother are able to smoothly go through passport control. Soon they are picking up their bags and are sitting in a taxi.

Somalia and its people have been independent for nearly thirty years. Although they had been living under a military dictatorship, which Farah noticed through all of the posters of the president around them since they landed in the airport, the Mogadishans seemed a lot more cosmopolitan than what he had expected.

"It is very nice here," he says to his mother, who looks at him like she had told him so.

The truth of the matter was that this young man had never been to Africa. The only Africa Farah knew was the one he had seen on television in London, the one who he had heard about people speak so nostalgically while they fled for all sorts of reasons, the one the young man never thought he would visit until his mother's nagging desire to visit her country forced him. He was the youngest, the unmarried, and the one who had the responsibility of accompanying his aging and fragile mother. Farah did not understand why his mother had such a deep longing for her homeland, even though the dictator had recently ravaged through her hometown of Hargeisa in the north. He didn't understand why Mogadishu, which the mother had briefly lived for a few years before she went to Europe with her diplomat husband, would suffice—a conflict in Farah's eyes, as he had seen her wail over what happened in the Somali north.

No, Farah did not know Africa. He didn't understand the hold it had over those who were born and bred in it, whose lungs first tasted the African air, and who had the privilege of drinking raw milk as fresh as the very things they saw.

Abdi, the driver Farah's mother's old friend had sent, was able to show the various parts of the city on their way to the hotel in the Xamar Bile neighborhood. They passed by the central market, the beach, and the many offices of the city center. Neighborhoods like Waaberi, Xamar Jajab, and Bondheere were things he had heard from his mother all of his life. Now, here he heard it from Abdi as they drove by.

At Liido Beach, the city's most beloved beach, Abdi stopped the car for a little bit to let the travelers get some real breeze.

"Oh, my God," said Farah, as he got out of the car, his mouth dropped, and his eyes widened and with a big smile on his face.

The young man was immediately in love. This was the Africa he had never known he had wanted to come to. It was better than the posters he would see around London that advertised holiday destinations in southern Europe. Here the water looked far more natural, as the African morning sun hit the Indian Ocean. Whereas the beachgoers in those posters were mostly non-Black Europeans, which always made him feel like an outsider or something that just was not meant for him, the people at this beach mostly looked like him. Farah saw young men like himself run around, playing soccer. He saw beautiful women dip their feet into the water, laughing joyously. He saw children far in the distance, unafraid of their deep blue sea.

"Jesus," he murmured.

Yes, he was immediately in love. It was going to be his spot. The young man knew instinctively that he would go back. He felt in his bones, as sudden as that breeze hitting his face just minutes before, that there was something in Mogadishu for him. The young man wasn't sure exactly what it was, but there was a feeling that suggested there was indeed something. It was a feeling he could not shake all the way to the hotel, as they checked into their rooms, and as he and his mother enjoyed a Mogadishan breakfast through their room service.

"Oh, what an absolute delight," his mother smiled very happily, as she took a bite, her eyes closed as if she had just been transported to another time.

The fresh goat liver was precisely what she needed. It was perfectly sautéed in a bed of vegetable oil, onions and bell peppers. They served *canjeelo*, the flatbread, along with it. Farah never had it this fresh, and he too was enjoying his breakfast.

"I will take a little nap," said his mother,

after they finished.

His mother had not slept even for a minute in the entire ten-hour flight. The poor woman was exhausted, primarily since it was an overnight trip. Farah knew she would be out for some time. It was just past nine in the morning, and now he could dash off to the beach.

CHAPTER 2

I knew something magical was going to happen that day. I knew it before I opened my eyes. The whitewashed walls of our house were already filled up with scents and sounds. Spices from the street food, the neighbor ladies squabbling in several languages over their laundry lines, the barks of abandoned dogs and everywhere the whistling wind bringing the desert sand through our windows and doors. No nightmares, but I hadn't had any in weeks, so that didn't explain my wonderful mood. Something in the wind reminded me of my grandma.

She had been a wise one, my grandma. "Life is all about making decisions that don't exactly feel right to other people," she'd say. Then she would laugh at a fond memory and reach out to rub my thick black hair. "You are a brave one, Hanad. You should always choose what feels right, rather than what is expected."

It was exactly what I needed to hear as I stood in the middle of the road with a backpack full of school books. The wind brought the sharp scent of the ocean to me. On one hand I needed to get to school — but this urge! Grandma's wisdom surfaced at the right time in my memory for me to have the best day of my life.

"Hanad, shouldn't you be in school?" said my neighbor, who was two seats ahead of me.

For the life of me I could not remember his name. "I'm going to a swimming tournament," I lied. "It's at the Brazilian Embassy," I added, knowing he probably didn't even know where it was.

"Are you planning on leaving the country?"

"No," I chuckled, "I wish."

"We need all our young men in this country," he smiled confidently, "Don't dash off to a foreign country like your parents. Stay in school and do something with your life right here."

I nodded just to end to the conversation. He had no clue that I longed to follow my parents back to Italy. I spent my first 6 years there and still dreamt in Italian. Somalia was home, but it was dirty, corrupt and dysfunctional. And at least we had good food and well-traveled people. Everyone had a brother or an aunt that came visiting from somewhere else.

"Very well," he said, adding, "Good luck with your tournament."

"Thanks," I murmured, as I took out my Walkman and put on my headphones.

… Nomadi che cercano … Gli angoli della tranquillità … Nelle nebbie del nord … E nei tumulti delle civiltà …

As I listened to Franco Battiato, I began to think about what that man had said to me. Why would he discourage someone from going abroad? It occurred to me those rumors about him getting into legal troubles back in Russia were probably correct. Why else would he deny me an opportunity?

"So and so just returned from Russia," I remembered Jamilo, our great rumor mill ringleader in the neighborhood, saying to my mother. "I was not surprised to hear the authorities of that country are after him," she smiled mischievously, as she took a sip of her favorite spiced tea, "I heard he loves to bed European women."

I marveled how I could remember the details of the rumor, the rumor bearer, and yet not the name of the subject of such rumor.

"Next stop: Arbaca Rukun!"

The conductor interrupted my thoughts. I got off and tried to get another minibus. No such luck! The few that were running were full of morning commuters. A fellow driver had been killed by the Red Hat soldiers last week and many of the drivers were on strike. Just another day in our chaotic capital.

I began my twenty-minute walk to the beach. "Grandma," I looked up at the sky, "this better be worth it."

It must have been months since I was last at Liido Beach. I had forgotten how amazing the breeze was near the water like that. Even though it wasn't even ten in the morning yet, it was already scorching. I took off my shoes, felt the nice sand under my feet, closed my eyes, and breathed in the breeze.

I heard someone walking through the sand. I opened my eyes and saw the most delicious guy I've ever seen walking towards me. I guessed the guy was my age, 17, or a little older. He had muscles that stood out from his arms like those in the magazines I hid under my bed. His skin was smooth and flawless, hung with tiny drops of seawater that glistened like diamonds. I had the urge to lick one and see if his skin tasted like sweet milky coffee or chai tea. He was wearing a Speedo, not even a knockoff but the real thing, which made me think he was from the diaspora or maybe a tourist.

"Hi," I smiled at the beautiful sight before me.

I dared not look at his body, his crotch, his amazing legs—nothing. I was afraid I would jump on him. His face was just the type of face I liked. He had a strong jaw and a sharp nose, and yet there was so much sensitivity in his thickly lashed eyes.

"Hi," he smiled too, as if I was as cute as him. I had a slender body that older men enjoyed, but my best feature was my strong chin that kept my even features from being too feminine. "Have we met before?"

I wanted to say yes after seeing his beautiful smile, but I had used up my lies this morning skipping school.

"No," I replied. "I don't think so."

"Are you sure?"

"Is anyone ever sure about anything, really?"

He laughed. "You're right." Then he extended his hand to me. "I'm Farah."

"Hanad." I shook his hand. "Nice to meet you."

Farah, as I already calculated, was indeed from the diaspora. He had been born in Amsterdam where his father worked for the Somali Embassy, but his parents decided to move to London later. He said moving from Dutch-speaking to English-speaking country was not a big deal, mainly since he kept speaking Somali at home.

"My parents were adamant that I learn Somali first," he said. "By age five I could converse just like a child growing up here in Somalia."

"I'm the opposite," I told him. "My parents met and married in Italy, and they had me there, and when I was six we moved back to Somalia because my father wanted me to get my education here."

"Wow," he seemed surprised, "That is cool!"

I laughed, "Why?"

"In Britain they like Italian culture," he told me.

"Really?"

"Yeah, there are a lot of Italians in London," he said. "The Italian people seem to always be in favor, especially when it comes to beauty of art or people," he turned to me inquiringly. "Do you speak Italian?"

"Of course," I told him. "My parents only spoke to me in Italian. It was when we moved here that they began to teach me Somali, and the rest I learned naturally."

"It is really incredible how global our people are."

"That is what happens when you deal with colonialism, corruption, and dictatorship," I countered. "I would have preferred to have been born here, but only if it were a better country than we have now."

We kept sharing our lives and worldviews until it was lunchtime. I took him to Mama Roma Restaurant.

"What do you recommend?" he asked me.

As I began to answer, I realized one of my favorite songs was playing. "Ssshhh…" I said, listening, my eyes closed.

Bambino, Bambino ne pleure pas, Bambino…

"Les yeux battus la mine triste," I sang along. "Et les joues blêmes…"

"Who was that singer?" asked Farah, after it finished.

"You don't know Dalida?"

"Oh, yeah, I've heard of her," he said, although I could see from his face that he probably didn't. This marvelous artist wasn't very popular in Somali culture yet. "That sounded French."

"It was, mostly," I replied. "This is a song with as many lives as any good cat," I told him. "I'm aware of several renditions of it but there are probably more. The version by Dalida is a mix of French and Italian, although 'bambino' is the only Italian word in the song," I added. "However, the song was originally a traditional Neapolitan song." Farah gazed at me with so much interest. "I believe the original title was 'Guaglione,' which means a young boy, although it also has darker meaning of 'street children.' Dalida covered the song and it became her first hit. Because she was ethnically Italian it made better sense for her musical producers to include Italian references in the song that aren't in the original song. So, lines by writer Jacques Larue, such as 'que tout le ciel de l'Italie,' which means 'the sky of all of Italy,' are meant to accompany her foreign accent in French. Likewise, American singer Dean Martin did a rendition, even farther from the original story. In Martin's rendition it is about a playboy musician who can win you any girl for a glass of wine and a pack of cigarettes."

Farah's face lit up in amusement.

"It is music, you know, anyone can improvise." I shrugged. My friends would never let me ramble like that.

"So, which one is your favorite?"

"I actually like an Italian version by Renato Carosone the best." Farah widened his eyes in surprise. "I should say it makes me dance best. It includes whistles and things like that."

Farah leaned back. He was fully relaxed and into the discussion. "You seem to really know music history."

"Only the music I like," I chuckled. I went back to the menu and picked it up. "I'm hungry. What are you in the mood for?"

"I was hoping you would recommend—"

"Oh, yes," I interrupted him and looked at the menu.

"Pick something good!"

"I'm a simple guy and I always go with the *Baasto Reer Xamar*," I said. "They serve it with fish rather than the typical Pomodoro. If you don't add the '*Reer Xamar*' part they will just give you spaghetti with vegetables and meat," I added.

Farah raised his eyebrows.

"The *isbaramuunto* here goes well with that, too," I told him. "They use oranges that are not fully ripe just yet. And, of course, lots of sugar!"

"Yummy," he said, but he was looking at my lips. "So, how old are you?" he casually asked.

I hesitated over telling him the truth, but I was adamant about having used all my lies for the day. "I'm 17." I hoped he wouldn't get up and walk away.

"Nice," he said, licking his lip, which absolutely drove me crazy. I let him finish his thought instead. "You're a lot more mature than I am," he added.

"How old are you?"

"I'm 19," he smiled.

"Thank God," I laughed. "I have a 5-year rule. I can't be friends with anyone older than that and most certainly not anyone younger than me!"

His eyes crinkled in agreement. He reached for his glass and his backpack tumbled over. I picked up a book that fell out. "What is this? A novel! Is it gay?" I opened the first page.

"Yes," replied Farah, "I think it is gay."

I began to read. Farah took it back.

"You can read later," said Farah, not wanting to lose his new friend to the book just yet. "I will let you borrow it, don't worry."

I nodded.

"But only after lunch."

Lunch with Farah was absolutely fantastic. I found him to be utterly accessible as a person. I usually don't like to put so many questions to new people, but I was comfortable talking about everything with him.

I felt like we made a good connection.

We exchanged numbers, and we made plans to meet the following night, as he was already tied up that afternoon and evening with his ill mother.

As I went back home, in a very crowded *caasi*, I began to realize and appreciate that Grandma had come through in a big way.

"Thank you, Grandma," I whispered.

It was the best day I had had in a long time.

Of course, when I got home, everyone was out, and the house was as quiet as could be. I went to my room and I locked the door. Now I could allow myself to think about Farah. Now I could let myself to look at him the way I really wanted to look at him. I took off my shirt, my shorts, and I closed my eyes. I replayed the first moment I saw him when my eyes briefly scanned his everything.

I needed to be with him—fast.

CHAPTER 3

It was nearly a week until I had a gap between my mother's appointments long enough to meet at the beach again. Hanad was waiting for me eagerly. Our phone calls had been fun, but not enough.

I loved the way he spoke, the way he pronounced certain words. It was very different from the type of dialect I was used to at home and in my circle of Somali friends in London. His Xamari dialect was softer, much closer to Arabic than my own, which the natives of this city called Qaldaan, or "Incorrect."

"The Waqooyi is a beautiful dialect," I defended my mother tongue by its geographical name. "I know you got to be the seat of our united territories, which some of us still protest, but that doesn't mean your dialect is more correct."

Hanad laughed in surprise and asked rightfully, "Then why did you guys agree to have Mogadishu as your capital?"

"Because the Italians were nicer to you than the British were to us," I explained. "They built beautiful buildings here, old arches and churches, and they even got train systems for you," I added, repeating the type of comebacks I had heard all my life from my northern relatives. "Your city was just more of a capital on the surface than our beloved Hargeisa."

"What is Hargeisa like?"

"I heard it is very nice. It is the true capital of our people. I don't say that to offend you or anything, but it is home to all of the beautiful things our culture is known for like poetry, rock art, and indigenous tribes."

"Are you saying we don't have nice poetry or diverse tribes in Mogadishu?"

"In school here, whom do you learn about in your 'Soomali iyo Suugaan' course? Sayyid Mohammed Abdille Hassan, Ismail Mire, and Hadrawi," I added, watching his eyes widen, "These are all men from the North."

"You're right," he laughed. "I'm moving there!"

"No," I laughed, "Stay here. Our brightest minds already invested here. Whatever good Somalia there is today you will find in Mogadishu," I added. "Unless, of course, you count the many talented exiles who are chewing khat in London."

"God, I would love to live in London." Hanad romantically swept his eyes closed. "I would love to visit where Oscar Wilde lived, hold hands with someone on the streets without being looked down on, and—"

"First of all," I corrected him, "You can hold hands in Mogadishu and—"

"You know what I mean," he interrupted, smiling so beautifully.

"Right now, in February, London is very cold," I said to him, as a matter of fact. "You wouldn't dream of holding anyone's hand there. You would keep your hands warm in your pockets."

Then, he placed his hands on mine, and my fingers natural intertwined with his. "Your hands are not cold."

And we were too busy to speak for a little while. I liked the way my hand felt in his. Hanad's warm hands were now warming my entire body. My heart was beating and I could feel the sensual sensation of my being called out to the surface. I could feel he was feeling the same.

Hanad told me a bit more about his life. He talked warmly about his best friend, Roti. He said he could share anything with Roti.

"So, have you and Roti had sex?"

"Are you crazy?" Hanad looked taken aback, full of genuine shock, as he let go of my hand. "Roti is like my brother. I can't imagine things like that with him."

Then I felt embarrassed. I may be older, but I wasn't as sure what was normal. Keeping every fling and crush a secret didn't help. I longed to have a gay friend like Roti.

"But he is so fucking sexy," Hanad teased.

"He is?" I came out of my shell to narrow my eyes playfully.

"Oh, yeah," said Hanad. "I warn you that if you fall in love with him I will kill you both," he laughed. "You're all mine!"

I laughed too. He had forgiven me.

CHAPTER 4

Roti knew Hanad was probably having the best time of his life with that new guy, but he missed his best friend. Every time he stopped by the house Hanad was out, and the two times Hanad came by his home he wasn't there. It was as if they were living in parallel worlds.

"Where have you been all this time?" Roti barged into Hanad's room.

"Oh, Roti!" Hanad smiled dreamily at his best friend. His face made all sorts of cute expressions. "I think I died and went to heaven. I really—"

"What was it like?" asked Roti. He prepared his inner being for what he was to hear. "I need to know every detail!"

"Roti, you would never believe me!"

"Oh, try me!" Roti was dying to get the juicy details, which was not surprising at all to his friend Hanad, as Roti was known for his curiosity.

Hanad began to share all the things he had experienced. Roti was really shocked to hear all the emotional adventures Hanad has had. Hanad told him he thought he was in love already.

"Did you do it yet?"

"Sex?" asked Hanad.

"Duh! Yeah?"

"No," smiled Hanad, "Not yet."

"Hhmmm," squinted Roti, "I think something is fishy here." He stared into Hanad's eyes, looking for the answer. "You normally jump into bed first chance you get and now—"

"That is just it." Hanad looked a bit annoyed. "I hope you don't think I'm the devil, but I feel like he's spending all of his time with his mom. We never even have the time to be alone together."

"Wait, you haven't been alone yet?"

"No, we have. But at the beach, or at restaurants, or somewhere public." Hanad glanced away to hide his worried sad gaze. "I fear we won't have time before he returns to London."

"How soon is that?"

Hanad chewed on his lip. "A few more weeks I think. He isn't sure."

Roti crossed his arms. "Then I better meet him soon. Anyone who can make you this rattled I want to know."

After Roti had gone home Hanad discovered that novel from Farah in his backpack. The novel, entitled "Haji," was written by a Somali writer in the United States.

"Hhhmm," said Hanad.

The cover featured a camel being guided by a young nomad in *qayd*, the traditional Somali robes. The rider sat on a golden chair on top of the camel and was draped in elaborate, concealing layers of silk. Had it not been for the sword he worn across his body, Hanad would have assumed the rider was a woman.

What a beautiful cover, thought Hanad.

One could see the cover artist was very much into this piece, as so much detail was devoted to the artwork.

Hanad opened the book, went through the first pages, and just fell into the story…

Prologue

The letter arrived just after morning prayers, but it had not made it yet to the young sultan.

The wazir intercepted it.

He knew the content of the letter, as he had purchased the oral communication that had accompanied it.

The messenger of this letter had to travel on the Indian Ocean, from Zanj to Mogadishu, and the several sultanates that lay between them were not exactly known to be the most peaceful in the world. In case the letter was lost, or damaged its messenger would deliver the oral communication.

"'I will wait for you in Zanj,'" relayed the messenger, a young merchant from the Mali Empire who had accompanied Prince Bilal to Zanj. "'If you don't come in three months, I will return home and will resume my royal duties, as your absence would have me know you had done the same yourself. But, please, come.'"

Now the young wazir was torn.

On the one hand, he knew it was against his beliefs to keep a message from its intended recipient. This was mainly the case since he knew that the love the prince had felt for the sultan was most surely reciprocated. The sultan was his friend, and he knew very well he was genuinely in love.

On the other hand, the young wazir knew if the message was delivered it could lead to chaos at best. The wazir knew Farah very well and knew the young sultan would have left for his lover, and the abdication would make everyone question the honor of the royal family.

In another scenario, however, the young wazir knew the situation could end up far worse. The abdication could lead to the infighting of the brothers, over who would be the next sultan, and that could make the sultanate vulnerable to takeovers by the neighboring enemies.

The young wazir, sitting on the edge of the bed, nervously made his decision.

The rest would be up to Allah.

Hanad was most enchanted by this prologue and wanted to read more, but he decided to take in the story very slowly. It was like a treat you didn't want to finish too fast. Of course, he didn't know anything about the story, but Hanad knew it was fascinating just from reading the prologue. So, he put the book away and went for a walk—to visit his favorite coffee shop.

That evening Hanad was able to speak to Farah on the phone.

"I would love to meet Roti, too," said Farah.

"How about tomorrow for dinner?"

"Oh, man!" said Farah. "Tomorrow afternoon my mom and I are going to Afgooye. It is a big thing for her. Actually, it is the real reason we came. She will visit some sort of a spiritual healer. We probably won't be back until late that evening."

Disappointed, Hanad sighed heavily into the phone.

"I'm sorry," said Farah, his voice as sweet as Hanad ever heard it, "I know I'm not as available as I should be. I'm asking you to have patience with me."

Then they were both silent for a second.

"I want you to know that I would love to be with you every moment of my day," said Farah, which made Hanad feel all warm inside and put a huge smile on his face. "I want to be with you more than anyone in this world."

"Really?"

"Yes, really," said Farah.

Hanad loved the way he felt hearing that. It was as though something in him was healing. He felt he needed that after all the heartbreaks in his young life. It was really vital for him to know he was so important to Farah. It did away with any doubts he had.

He smiled so ever brightly.

CHAPTER 5

Barni, accompanied by her son Farah and her best friend Saredo, arrived at the home of Isnino Abukar in Afgooye. She had been looking forward to meeting Isnino, as she believed her very life depended on the spiritual healer's help. This wasn't something Barni had come upon overnight. No, this idea was planted in her years before. It was at a time when her younger sister Asli was very ill. The doctors had given up on Asli but it was Saredo who finally got her to Isnino. The visit to Isnino immediately relieved all of Asli's symptoms.

Asli, it turned out, was suffering from an acute case of possession. It was something residing in her for decades. It was traced back to a lover she rejected. Asli was only sixteen when she had met the older, stable, and most suitable Sayid. The man had recently returned from London and all of Hargeisa was wooing him. Everyone who had an unmarried daughter, sister, or friend tried to get him to their daughter, sister, or friend. It was said that a photograph of the young Asli, which was unintentionally shown to Sayid by Asli's uncle, stole the man's heart. Much to everyone else's surprise, however, the young woman said she did not want to marry Sayid. She had other ideas. So, claimed Isnino, Sayid had visited a witch and she placed *sixir*—black magic—in the young Asli.

"Oh, Barni, she even knew his name," said Asli at the time, as the accuracy of the spiritual healer shocked her. "From the first visit I felt my pain ease a whole lot. By the third visit I no longer was in pain. It is a miracle!"

Yes, Barni had been dreaming of visiting Isnino for a long time. Now she too had her chance and she intuitively felt everything would be alright. All she needed was to see her and she knew a prescription would make itself known.

"*Bi'idnillahi karim*," whispered Barni, praying for God's will.

After waiting for about four hours Barni was finally in front of Isnino. They studied one another. Barni was surprised to see that Isnino was a lot younger than she had imagined. Sure, she never asked how old the woman was, but Barni never expected to meet a woman in her early forties. Isnino had a square face that immediately reminded Barni of a woman she had known back in Hargeisa. The only difference was that that woman happened to be a few decades older, had more wrinkles, and life had generally worn her out a bit more. Isnino, on the other hand, was together. She had light brown eyes, which perfectly complemented her fair skin tone. Her nose was wide, as wide as any good West African, and her hair, of which Barni could see only the front, was kinkier than the typical Somali woman. Her lips were full and when she spoke they slowly parted to reveal strong teeth—a smile much larger than anyone Barni had ever known. From head to toe Isnino was wrapped in *shaash* silk. Barni thought it was odd since this material was usually reserved for the head of newly married women. She had never seen anyone wear a full garment out of it, though she liked it immensely.

Isnino, however, was not as taken with Barni as Barni seemed to be with her. To Isnino Barni was just a normal Somali lady. She had seen plenty of them. She had also seen plenty of them react to her the same way Barni reacted. Their mouths would open at first sight of Isnino, their eyes would follow her for a while, and finally their questions would begin.

"I'm Bajuni," she would tell these women. "Not all of us come from the Bajuni Islands. I come from Kismayu. I was born in Calanleey, the oldest part of town, as were my mother and her mother and all of our women for thousands of years. We changed names in different parts of history, sure, but who we are stayed the same."

If she really, really felt comfortable with them, which often was not the case, she would let them in on the family secret. She would say her grandmother had an affair with a young man from northern Italy. She would tell them that her mother was not really the biological daughter of the man who raised her as his own. It was an open secret, which, Isnino would add, was how she got to be so light skinned.

"I, on the other hand, was born in a Muslim marriage," Isnino would smile.

After all, she wouldn't want any good Muslim woman to worry about making spiritual deals with a woman who came into the world as a bastard child. God knew it was hard enough to be talking about things they could not see, even if they believed.

Barni turned out to be one of those lucky ones who got the full story.

"What a fascinating biography," responded Barni.

Now that she satisfied Barni's natural curiosity about her, which she felt comfortable she satisfied, Isnino turned to Barni's real reason for coming. She asked the sickly woman what was the problem. Barni pointed to her midsection and head and she said she would alternate in pain in those areas, although the midsection seemed to be the one with the longest and most acute of the pains she had suffered.

"Relax," said Isnino, as she placed her hands over Barni's midsection. "I will only gently push," she added, doing just that. "If you feel anything you let me know."

In the meantime, while slightly pushing Barni's midsection, Isnino closed her eyes. She began to chant something Barni, her son, or her friend did not understand. It sounded to them as if it were a language of the Swahili people.

"Oh, yes," finally said Isnino, as she sat back.

Barni and her entourage looked on.

"I suspected it when you walked through the door," said Isnino, confidently grinning, "I thought I recognized that aura, but I had to be sure, you know?"

No one knew what she was talking about.

"You must have used to gather wood for cooking," said Isnino, watching Barni's eyes widen.

"Yes," smiled Barni. "When I was a little girl. How did you know?"

"It is the usual way girls stumble upon Ash," said Isnino.

Barni nodded, even though she didn't know who or what Ash was. Isnino explained. She said it was the Egyptian God of nature, especially any kind of oasis or vineyards around the Nile. To the Somali, however, Ash was the head of a tribe of Jinn whose function in the world is to guard trees, especially young or old trees.

"Since girls seek out old or dried up trees, as it is easier to gather wood, they often break a brunch in which one of Ash's tribesmen might be guarding," explained Isnino.

It was in that moment that Barni recalled one particular early evening when she had experienced something very strange. She was gathering wood when suddenly a rush of cold air swept over her young body. Isnino confirmed it was usually how this type of possession was described by the many women who came to seek her help in the matter.

"It is a simple process to resolve it," said Isnino.

Isnino went on to explain to Barni that normally people went through five stages of healing. In the first stage, or what Isnino called *dabqaad*, a small offering would be made. The offering would be made so that one of Ash's tribesmen can be summoned. There was a particular one that Isnino worked with for similar cases and she was confident he would show up. Isnino would tell the Jinn that in exchange for easing Barni's symptoms that they were committed to go through other stages such as *samrad*, *nus mingis*, *muul*, and *calaqad*—stages that would build up their offerings to the final stage, which would give the said Jinn a large animal.

"For now, we only need to give coffee and beans," said Isnino.

Sure enough everything Isnino said turned to be exactly as she had described it. The Jinn easily showed up, although only Isnino could hear or see him. *Qaxwo* and *bun* was offered in exchange for his supernatural presence. He agreed to the offering stages Isnino presented.

That evening Barni went back to her hotel. She was feeling better than she had felt in many years. There was an easiness in Barni that reminded her of what her sister Asli had told her all those years ago.

"It is working," she smiled to herself.

CHAPTER 6

The green was unlike any green Hanad had ever seen. He was lying on his back, the grass under his bare body, and he liked the way the mixture of dirt and grass felt to his skin. It was cooler, too, which gratified his warm body under the African heat. Hanad watched all the different greens around him. There were mango trees, papaya trees, banana trees, and there were even trees he didn't know what type of fruit they offered.

"Wow," said Hanad, as his eyes widened.

He could smell all the fragrance oozing out of these trees. He turned his head to his left side and saw a lot of fallen leaves, and he picked up one and brought it to his nose to smell. It smelt like a cloud of perfume from a faraway land. He closed his eyes, and it was as though he saw a mountain surrounded by a forest with children, happy and free in the distance.

It was that very moment that Hanad felt hands creeping up on his body. First, they were on the legs, and then they were caressing his torso, and now they were firmly massaging the shoulders. Hanad could also feel the breath of the person on his neck—soft and warm. He felt the touch of his lover's lips on his neck. The lips were parted, and the tip of the tongue's wet presence was now on Hanad's neck. Hanad didn't have to think twice; he knew it was Farah. He slowly turned his head and, as the two faces brushed against one another, Hanad opened his eyes.

He opened his eyes in the dream and in the real world. He was alone in his bed. He immediately closed his eyes again, as he desperately wanted to get back to that dream. He never wanted to wake up from that dream. Suddenly, however, his questions about "why" and "how" he woke up distanced Hanad from the dream and planted him more and more in the real world.

"*Cazzo!*" he murmured, cursing in Italian as naturally as ever, and opened his eyes again.

For the rest of the day, no matter where he was or what he was doing, Hanad was haunted by that dream. Immediately after waking up, and even before he brushed his teeth, he called Farah. They talked for a few minutes, and finally, Hanad asked his new friend if he was available for lunch.

"Oh, I would love that," said Farah, with a sigh. "I think I won't be able to, though," he added.

"I have to take my mother to the house of another relative today."

"I know you're there for your mother," said Hanad, empathically. "You take care of her. You're a good son, and that is a good thing."

"I just wish it wasn't taking all of my time," complained Farah, "Today is such a long day for me. We probably won't be back from these relatives until near dinner time, as they live in Shalaambood. And then for dinner, we are meeting the family for dinner at my aunt's house."

Hanad listened to his friend, and he tried to be as understanding as he could. Despite his need to see Farah, which at that moment was more intense than ever before, Hanad also understood that he would need to be patient.

Frustrated, Hanad spent a lot more time under the cold shower that morning than he normally would. Some of his cousins knocked on the door, trying to start their mornings, but the young man was just not hearing any of it. He was as heedless about the insults hurled at him later for taking up all of that bathroom time.

"Aren't you going to eat?" asked the maid. She tried to mother him a bit, with his parents in Italy half the year and his grandma gone these past few years.

Breakfast was the last thing on his mind, as all his energy and thoughts were squarely resting on either the dream or the lack of time with his new man. They were so interchangeable—in and out, one leg in the vision and the other in the real world—that hunger just never rose in him that morning.

He arrived at school a bit too early, which was usually not the case, but it gave him a chance to read that novel. He took the book out of his backpack and began reading it. He escaped from his own dreams to fall into someone else's.

Dardaaran

Farah stood over his father's lifeless body. It all seemed to have gone so fast, he thought. Just a few minutes earlier the *wadaad* was here to give his father the last rites. The boy had watched, as the sheikh read the final verses of Yaa Siin. Yaa Siin, the 36th chapter or surah of the Qur'an, is believed to carry the individual into the next world because it presents all of the important themes of the Book.

The boy knew his father had been ill. He had been sick for a long time, actually. He has had plenty of close calls over the previous several months. And even that morning, when he walked into his father's bedroom, the boy thought he smelled death in the air.

Yet, somehow, the boy felt it was sudden.

The death of his father was more than just any death. In the boy, a core belief was broken. His father was just another human being, after all. He was not a god.

At the same time, the boy was prepared for this moment. His father had made sure he had gone through every training the young boy would need, and the old man was confident he had made the right decision entrusting his legacy in his sixteen-year-old hands.

In his final days on Earth, when he was sure death was around the corner, the old man had talked to the boy. He had his *dardaaran* with him.

"If someone comes to you," he told his son, with as much strength as he could muster, "If they say to you that your father owed them something," he continued, as the boy listened, attentively, "Don't believe them. I don't owe anyone anything."

The father had talked to his son about this many months earlier. However, certain things needed to be repeated. For example, he reminded his son to make the Hajj on his behalf, and soon. He knew life gets in the way, as it did with him, and he wanted his son to have the chance to fulfill one of his father's oldest dreams.

"I will do it," Farah had replied.

"Do it this coming year," the old man said.

But now his father was gone. He would go to as many pilgrimages as was needed to keep him alive. He thought if he could have one more year with him, just one more year, he would be more prepared.

"Nonsense," was the thought that came to him, in the voice of his father, as the morning chill brushed against his wet cheeks, "No one is ever prepared. Life is life, and it does not wait for anyone. It goes on."

He wiped the tears from his face. He covered his father's body, after kissing his forehead one last time, and left the room.

The sheikh was waiting outside. He did not go into the rest of the house, as he knew many people were waiting for news. He wanted the son to inform the people, and he did not want to lie.

Together they walked the halls and reached the center of the home, where family members and friends were gathered.

"From God we come, and to Him we return," the boy said, as he heard himself say words he dreaded for so long and watched a calamity befall his people.

His mother, the wife of his father, was the strongest amongst the women. All of the ladies were crying except her. The faces of his brothers were stricken with sadness. He saw relatives and friends grieve.

"You're the sultan now," said Bashi, one of his uncles, "We are all looking to you for guidance," he added, as he kissed his nephew on the cheek. "I know my brother believed in you, and I believe in you as well."

Later that morning, the young sultan was visited by his most senior wazir. Warsame had been his childhood friend. They attended the madrassa together as children. Their fathers were as close as they themselves were now later in life.

Warsame was a slim and round-faced young man, with two large eyes and a long nose to match them. He had always been special to the sultan.

From age nine to age fourteen, when the young wazir married his first cousin, they had been lovers.

The previous year, as the sultan prepared for his post, their friendship became more official, more formal, and much less about their feelings.

"Thank you," said the young sultan, as his friend had hugged him tightly.

"I'm sorry about uncle," said Warsame, tears in his eyes.

The young sultan wiped the tears from his friend's face, and kissed him on the cheek.

"We are all grieving," he said, as they hugged again.

After a long hug, Warsame stood back, as he could feel they were crossing boundaries he was afraid would complicate things.

"The coronation will start soon," Warsame told his friend.

"I wish we didn't have to do this now."

"Your father was a great sultan," Warsame said, getting closer once more, caressing his friend's hand, "I know you agree he deserves to be buried by a sultan rather than just another son."

Farah knew his friend was right.

Hanad stopped reading at that point. He was surprised the main character in the novel he was reading was named Farah. Perhaps that is why his Farah's friend had given him the novel? Hanad wanted to read more but soon he would get to class, and he didn't want to stop in the middle. Besides, he was being haunted by that dream and he felt he just wasn't enjoying the read the same way.

CHAPTER 7

At school, everyone noticed the changes in Hanad. He was no longer the cheery boy he had been. Instead, he was more in his head than in the real world. The teachers would talk to him, and he would be absent-minded. Everyone knew that Hanad was never really good at math, but his favorite teacher—a tall and demanding Mr. Oodle, who taught the kids *Soomaali iyo Suugaan*—a course focusing on the Somali culture—noticed an even lower drop in Hanad's participation.

"What is happening with you?" Mr. Oodle asked after the class was dismissed.

"Nothing," he replied, looking away.

"Are your parents alright?"

"Yes," replied Hanad.

"Are they still working in Italy?"

"Yes," replied Hanad.

"When will they come back?"

"They still have two more months."

"And your cousins and aunt? Your uncle?"

"Everyone is okay."

"So, why are you acting so strange?"

Hanad didn't know what to reply.

"Did you meet a girl or something?"

"What?" Hanad was startled.

"Are you in love?"

Hanad looked down, embarrassed.

"Hhhmm," Mr. Oodle, studied the boy.

Mr. Oodle could see that he had finally pinpointed his student's malady. He was more than a teacher to the boy. He and Hanad's father, Mursal, were childhood friends. Mr. Oodle had fond memories of the time he and Mursal spent together running through the city. They had tried to keep in touch when Mursal went to Italy, but their weekly phone calls nearly vanished when Mursal married Hodan.

Nevertheless, the bond they shared withstood time. When Mursal returned to the country with his young family over a decade later they resumed their friendship as if no time had passed at all. Until it came time for Mursal to leave, as he did every spring. It was like that for years until one day Mursal brought more responsibilities to his friend, as Mursal wanted to bring his fourteen-year-old son to Muuse Galaal Secondary School.

"I want you to teach him everything you know," Mursal said, as looked around his friend's classroom.

"My class is Somali and Culture," noted Sahal. "I will teach him these subjects to the best of my ability, but a boy needs more. I think—"

"Why is it always about you?" asked angry Mursal.

"It is not about me, it's about Hanad," said Sahal in a low flat voice he had never used with his friend before. "I know you will continue to go back and forth to Italy, and I know you have to make a living, but I'm worried it will have negative effects on the boy. It was one thing to leave when your mother was still alive, but this year is different."

"That is why I'm bringing him here," said Mursal. "That is why I bought that house, far from our childhood neighborhood, because I wanted him to go to the school where you are. The boy needs you. I need you. Can't you see that?"

Sahal knew it was a bad idea, but he didn't want to punish the son for the sins of the father. Now here he was couple of years later, and he could see what he feared had happened. He worried Hanad would not pass his last year of secondary school and he would see history repeat itself. Hanad would end up leaving school and working abroad, just like his father.

"Can I go now?" asked Hanad, interrupting Mr. Oodle's dark musings.

"Not yet," said Mr. Oodle. He went to the back of the classroom and picked out what seemed to Hanad a hardcover book. He handed it to Hanad. "I too was once in love at your tender age. I poured all my feelings in here," said Mr. Oodle, as Hanad opened the book to discover it was just all plain pages and realized it was indeed a journal. "Love can consume you if you allow it."

"This is empty." Hanad looked up at his teacher with a surprised face.

"Yes, I tore out all the pages," Mr. Oodle gave a bittersweet smile. "I hope you didn't expect to read my most inner thoughts. I'm giving you this because I want you to make your own entries in it."

"I never had a journal before."

"It is okay," reassured Mr. Oodle. "I want you to go to your favorite place in the city and write a letter to your lover. Tell your love what you really are feeling. Be honest in your letter," Mr. Oodle continued, as Hanad nodded. "When you finish, tear it out of the journal, and burn it."

After school that day Hanad went straight to the beach, and he did precisely what Mr. Oodle had said. He wrote to Farah. His first letter was very simple, and yet it was so powerful to the young man. He wrote:

My Dearest Farah,
I love you. I love

you. I love you. I love you. I love you. I love you. I love you. I love you. I love you.

Love, Hanad.

He wrote so many letters that he ran out of the pages by the end of the day. He shared with Farah every single thing he could think of: his desires, his feelings, his fears, his hopes, everything. Hanad was as honest as he knew how. By that evening he realized why Mr. Oodle had given him the journal. He learned that by putting down his thoughts on paper he found some relief from the constant anxieties he was feeling. This practice was exactly what he needed. Now he could go back to the real world. He could get back to his family, his friends, his education, and his life in general.

On the way back, Hanad opened the novel…

Coronation

It was six years earlier when Farah's father spoke to his young boy about his future. The boy would never forget it. It happened just after Qur'an school, mid-morning. He had fallen asleep on the chair, and his father had gently awakened him.

"Come," he said to his son, "I want to talk to you."

The young boy followed his father, as they walked through the house, and into his father's favorite room.

The old man sat on the edge of the bed and motioned for his son to come and sit next to him.

Farah sat where he was told to sit.

He was nervous.

Very nervous.

"Many years ago," said the father, as he caressed his son's hair, "My father sat me in this room," he added, as he looked around the massive room that was his bedroom.

Farah looked up at his father.

"Anyway," said the father, getting back to his original story, "My father sat me down here and told me what I will tell you now. That moment changed my life. It is a moment I will never forget."

Then, just like that, the man got up and went to the window. He was silent for a little bit, looking out of that window as though he was looking back into the past. It was as if he could see that day, that moment, on the blue sky.

"Father, are you going to die?" asked Farah.

The father, laughing, said, "No." He always loved how aware his son was about the world around him. He knew none of his other sons would have asked him a question like that, as the thought would not have even crossed their silly minds. "No," he added, as he walked back to the bed, sitting once again next to his son, "I'm not dying. You're becoming alive. I'm choosing you as my heir to the throne," he smiled.

Farah was young, and he didn't honestly know exactly what his father was saying, but he knew the moment was significant.

"Okay," replied Farah. "But I have a question."

"Ask me," said the father.

"Why are you choosing me?"

"On the day you were born I felt something," said the father, "I felt something extraordinary. It was something I never felt with any of the other births of my children. But it was later, much later, when I knew you would be the one. You were probably four or five at the time. You sat on my lap, and you cleaned my shawl with your hand. You saw pieces of the leaves from the tree under which I had my meeting earlier that morning."

Farah seemed happy his father remembered that moment, even though he could not.

"What that moment told me was that you are the type of man who will continuously clean his people," said the father. "That type of a man is a leader."

Farah remembered that conversation as if it took place the day before. He recalled that discussion as the elders of his people took turns to pour milk all over him.

"May you live long, my sultan," each of the elders would say, as they would pour the milk.

Even though he had been acting as the sultan for the better part of the previous year, Farah was actually becoming a sultan for the first time at that moment.

The ceremony did not last long.

In an hour he was officially the new sultan.

Hanad was really enjoying this story. He looked around and realized he was not even half way to his house. Besides, he knew the conductor and he would be told when they reached his stop. So, he continued reading...

Burial

Sultan Aweys was to be buried that afternoon. He was to be buried according to his Muslim beliefs, which required that a male from his immediate family lead the washing of his corpse, be part of the burial prayers, and take him into the ground. Sultan Aweys had done the *meyt-dhaq*, *janaso*, and *butdhig* for his own father, and he would have expected the new sultan of his people to do the same.

No one ever teaches you to do this kind of thing, and young Farah had never had the chance to do such a thing. His father was the first person in his immediate family who had died in his entire life, and he wondered if he was up to the challenge.

The young sultan decided his father's body would be washed in the room he had died in, his favorite place, which was the room he slept in when he was at the palace. Farah would lead the washing, supported by his brothers, and uncle Bashi would guide.

"Remove all the clothing, but make sure to cover his private parts," Bashi instructed Farah, who followed his uncle's direction.

First, the body had to be emptied. Bashi and his brothers had to lift up the body just a little, and Farah was instructed to apply pressure to the stomach of the dead body. This was to allow the discharge to complete.

Afterward, the private parts had been washed the way the person would when he would have gone to the bathroom.

Once Bashi felt it was done correctly, Farah had to give ablution to the body. Rosewater was used to provide the body with a sweeter scent, and the orifices had been plugged with soft fabrics.

A white fabric, clean and serene, a *kafan*, had been wrapped around the body of the late sultan, and now it was ready for burial.

Farah remembered something his father had told him, and his eyes widened, and a small, sad smile came upon his lips.

"Father wanted a private burial," he said, tears setting in his eyes.

"Yes, he told me, also," agreed Bashi.

"So it shall be done."

The men then went to the royal cemetery, just behind the palace, where the sultans of the past had been buried, and they all agreed upon the plot the late sultan had picked out while he was alive.

Farah oversaw the grave of his father being dug up by the gravediggers.

Everything was being done quietly.

The public had been told they needed to observe a six-hour ban on public movement, and they followed. There was no one on the streets, and the city was as though it had been the dwelling of the ghosts.

Therefore, the funeral was going to be very quiet, and very private.

Even the royal women and children were not allowed to participate.

As the body of his father was lowered into the ground, Farah remembered Bashi's instruction to untie the white cloth on the side of the body that touched the Earth.

After the burial, on the way home, the boy asked his uncle if he had done an acceptable job. Bashi placed his arm over his nephew's shoulders, and he whispered to him that he did an excellent job and added that he was proud of him.

Farah was devastated his father had died, but a small smile came to his lips, knowing he had fulfilled all the duties of a royal son.

He was finally satisfied.

This story was becoming interesting for Hanad. However, he realized he wouldn't have time to read another chapter before he would get off the mini bus. So, he stopped reading. Of course, his mind immediately went back to that dream. He closed his eyes for the few minutes he had left and went over the dream again.

But he was getting sexually excited!

Who would get up for him now?

It was a bad idea to do that!

Oops!

CHAPTER 8

Hanad was pleased to hear from Ayanle, and even more excited about the party invitation. "I'm playing at an ambassador's house tomorrow. There will be lots of interesting people there. You can be my guest, and Roti too, of course," offered Ayanle.

"I'm actually seeing someone. Can I bring my boyfriend?"

"Sure! Make sure you bring your IDs."

"Is that producer still hovering around you?"

Ayanle chuckled, "I think he finally got the message."

"Remind me, why don't you want to be famous? I really don't get it!"

"Our culture doesn't appreciate music," Ayanle told his young friend. "Like most of our artists, I would not be making enough money as a musician. I would be devastated if I had to collect public funds to survive. It's just not my thing. I prefer to earn a real living elsewhere."

Ayanle was doing precisely what he believed. No one would say his life as an artist was easy. He always had a job, even though some of these jobs were not exactly the best, but he loved his jobs for the mere fact that they allowed him to do his art. His current job was a perfect example, as he worked long hours at the factory as a manager of a large unit. On his off days he was totally engulfed in his music.

Ayanle was 29, but you couldn't tell looking at him. He looked and acted like he was 19. He had a face the boys compared to the singer Prince. When he smiled you would see his perfect teeth, which he credited to his mother pulling the old ones out on time when he was a kid. He was six feet tall and must have weighed no more than 150 pounds. He wasn't as skinny as Hanad accused him of, but he could definitely stand to gain some.

Five years earlier Hanad's older brother, Mohammed, died in a car accident. Mohammed and Ayanle had been best friends, and Ayanle had taken over as the older brother ever since. He included Hanad in his social life, which meant he had to include Roti too, as the boys were inseparable.

Hanad couldn't reach Farah, so he dialed Roti's number.

"Another one of Ayanle's gigs," groaned Roti. "I'm afraid to ask around about this ambassador. He must be the ambassador to Nowhere."

Hanad laughed when he heard that. "It's got to be better than that party in Waxaracadde."

"Where four taxi drivers refused to take us? I guess we will never know, since we couldn't get there."

Hanad twisted his hand in the cord. "We might have trouble getting into this one too. Ayanle said they only allow guests who are over 18, which is so dumb," he grumbled, "since we have been going to parties since we were 11."

Roti was more philosophical, "Foreign missions have to be careful when they serve alcohol in this country. It is tough enough when you are dealing with the same government, not a new revolution every spring. Besides, I know where we can get just the thing to solve this."

It was just past sunset when Hanad and Roti arrived at the massive Bakaaraha market. It was the chaos hour. The day people were closing up while the night shift folks were just starting to arrive. Crisscrossing people, yelling people, and a lot of havoc in the air. The young men began looking for Cabdalle Shideeye, a guide to the black market. They had never gotten anything forged before and had no idea how to go about it. Sure, they pretended to be tough, but to those who looked at their perfect skin knew they are just good kids. They also looked clueless. They asked around, and the people seemed to be suspicious of them. No one offered any helpful information for fear that these boys would be working with the authorities. Finally, they found someone who was willing to help them—and as usual at the Bakaaraha—for a fee.

The good thing about Cabdalle Shideeye was that he had been cloned. He was no longer just one dude. There were literally hundreds of him in the market. They could do any illegal activity you wanted. He could be Ahmed, Hassan, or even Hussein at home—and their families might even believe they had legitimate businesses—but in Bakaaraha they were all Cabdalle Shideeye. The young men found their prices too high.

"If I get caught I will spend months in prison," said the first *mukhalas*, a forger, who quoted them $250. He wasn't bargaining, either.

"What is going on?" Roti asked. "My older brothers had fake IDs all over the place, and I know they didn't pay $250."

They spent more than an hour trying to find someone who was willing to work for less than $100. It was exhausting.

"How much?" asked Roti.

"$150," replied the forger, who would later introduce himself as Jamal.

"Forget it," said Roti and the young men began to walk away. They couldn't afford that much to go to one party.

"Wait," Jamal walked after them. "Make me an offer. I know where to get what you need."

"$25," offered Roti.

"$100," countered Jamal.

"No," said Hanad, as a matter of fact. "We will find someone else."

"Give me $75," said Jamal, his face as strong as any businessman at that market, "I will make the IDs for $75 and get you a visa for half the normal price. Anywhere in Europe. That is my final offer."

Hanad and his friend looked at each other—they knew they were not going to get a better deal than that. Hanad nodded. The man took the boys back to his shop.

"Can you really get a visa?" Hanad asked.

"We don't need a visa," Roti rolled his eyes.

"I can get a visa faster than anybody!"

Jamal was confident.

The boys didn't say anything.

"And what country shall I get the visa for?"

Roti knew Hanad would not pause for a second once he heard that.

"Can you get a visa for Italy?" Hanad asked.

The ambassador's house was a large white villa at the end of a cul-de-sac, surrounded by other large villas. Cars were double parked—and sometimes even triple parked—on the little street.

"I can't go any farther," said Dadirow, Roti's older brother who had given them a ride. "You're going to have to walk."

Grateful, the boys made their way to the house by zigzagging through the parked cars.

Part of Hanad wished Farah had accepted his invitation. He understood for Farah his mother came first, but it also wasn't lost on him that it was the third time he tried to invite him to something that the new friend didn't take up the offer.

"Whatever," he whispered, as they walked into the ambassador's house. He shook off the negativity he was feeling about it all.

The party was everything Ayanle had predicted. It was fun and full of cool people. It was the right mix of people. Sure, there were some boring diplomatic folks. The boys noticed some even wearing suits, which they thought was the ugliest thing to wear to a party. However, they also saw there were many young people, children of the diplomats and their friends. So, you could go to an area, and it would be boring political conversations, but just the next group could be fun young people discussing the latest hit songs of Madonna or gossiping about the dating lives of their friends.

"I'm feeling this. Thanks for the invite, Ayanle," smiled Hanad.

"Thank you, guys." Ayanle reached out for a group hug. "I'm happy you could make it."

"For once you invited us to a decent party," Roti said, as he looked around the ambassador's colorful soirée.

"I'm glad you like it," said Ayanle. "I will sing in about ten minutes." He was nervous every single time they had seen him before a gig. "Wish me luck!"

Although they were often critical of his gigs, the boys never doubted his talents. Ayanle had the rare quality of a voice that made you wonder why such an artist was not better known. They had experienced his ability to woo crowds first hand since they were little, even before he took them under his wing, but they were often happy to see how well-received his talents were for people new to him.

"Why isn't he on the radio?" one lady whispered to her friend once, during one of his performance. "I would pay good money to see him in concert!"

Part of Ayanle's success was his business mind to deliver targeted performances to his audiences. For the ambassador's party he chose renditions of classic ballads. The songs gave the older people a chance to reminisce about their younger days, and their children could slow dance. Everyone was happy.

Deeqooy damac wanaageey…

Hanad and Roti danced and watched their friend do his thing. His voice was as good as the original singer of the song, a legend known to them as Tubeec.

By looking at Ayanle you would not be able to tell he had worked as many hours he had that week. He had worked for five days and at least 12 hours each of those days. Anyone would want to take their weekend off and put up their feet, but not him. He looked as chilled as the famous musicians. His face was full of pride and his voice on target. He had delivered another entertaining evening for a lucky group of Mogadishans.

"He's just so passionate," noted Roti.

Hanad nodded with tears in his eyes.

"Hey, Ayanle. Where is Bilan, your *kacaan*?" His girlfriend Bilan was always the first to arrive for Ayanle's shows, to the point that the boys would say she was as loyal as a revolutionary soldier.

Ayanle's face turned sour. "She won't be coming anymore."

Hanad was startled. They had been a happy, teasing couple the last time he saw them.

"Why not?"

Ayanle shrugged like he didn't care but his eyes said otherwise. "She's busy." He looked over Hanad's shoulder. "Excuse me, I've got to go talk to someone."

Something about that strange conversation bothered Hanad, as they returned to their homes. Dadirow, Roti's brother, was dropping off Hanad first and he and his brother would continue home. In the meantime, they noticed Hanad was physically with them but he was somewhere else otherwise.

"You seem kind of quiet," said Dadirow, through the rearview mirror, looking into the young Hanad's eyes.

"Yeah, Bro, what's up?" Roti was curios, too.

"Nothing," Hanad shook his head, although everyone else in that car could see something was definitely bothering him.

Where was she? Hanad thought.

After he was dropped off, Hanad quietly went to his room. He turned the lights on and put on some music. However, he was still thinking about Bilan. So, he knew reading that novel would transport him out of that thinking…

Inheritance

Sultan Aweys had four current wives and sixty-two children. Seventeen children were born to his first wife, a woman who had died in the childbirth of their last child together. They were only married for twenty-four years, and they had six twins. His second wife bore him nine children, and she died from a snakebite while she was six months pregnant with their tenth child.

The sultan married his third wife but she bore no children so he set her aside. The fourth wife had nineteen, and the fifth sixteen. Finally, he married Farah's mother, a cousin. Except for Asli, all of his wives had been women he married to strengthen political ties, as his father advised.

"Funny," he once told his brother Bashi. "I finally married a relative, and she bears a child that I think might take over the reigns."

"I think that was your intention," his brother chuckled, knowing his brother better than the brother knew himself. "I always knew you were meant to lead," he added, as he gave him that approving eye his brother cherished.

"You're a wise man," the sultan replied.

That was not how Bashi felt when he had to consult his nephew about how to go and divide the wealth the late sultan had left behind.

Of course, the *wadaad* had given the religious perspective on the subject. However, Bashi knew there was much room to roam when one was in charge of those entrusted with these positions.

"There are things that the sultanate needs," he told the sheikh, as they walked in the courtyard alone. "Sultan Farah, therefore, should manage the majority of the wealth for a specified time," he added, seeing the religious man was uneasy, "Just for a specified time until the sultanate can regain what it will lose in the inheritance."

A few days later, the new sultan gathered his relatives and informed them that they would all get about ten percent of what they are due to inherit.

Expectedly, many did not like this. Bashi had come to his nephew's defense and made a case for why such a thing was best for all of them. After all, if the sultanate's strength was weakened through inheritance then all of them could lose what they had gained.

In the end, the subjects had to go along with what the sultan had declared.

They all knew, from experience, that this was information shared, not a request.

While the family was dealing with their own questions of inheritance, one of the boys came in. There was a question that needed to be answered by the new sultan. The *qadi*, the Muslim religious judge, required a decision from the leader.

Farah looked at the piece of paper, and it said that a woman had accused her sons of killing their father so that they could have access to their inheritance sooner. Now, it came out, the woman is being charged with actually having been the one who committed the murder. Since neither side has any witnesses, the *qadi* felt this was a question to be decided by the sultan.

"A mother will not condemn her children to death," said the young sultan, and instructed the *qadi* to rule the inheritance to the state and not punish either of them.

As the messenger returned to the judge, the young sultan began to understand what it is like to have the life and death of subjects in one's discretion that way. Now he knew why his father had many sleepless nights, weighing the fates of his people.

He felt a small kiss in the wind, on his cheek.

He was not startled, nor was he afraid.

"Father," he touched his cheek.

Hanad didn't even think twice about reading another chapter. He just went right into it…

Hajj

Sultan Aweys had left many friends behind. He also left behind a few enemies, too. Sultan Ahmed, in the adjacent territory to the north, was one of his fiercest enemies. He believed that Sultan Aweys had a longer coastline than his own and that when the elders of the Somali had decided the borders, which took place hundreds of years before either of their birth, he was cheated.

As such, when he showed up on the shores of Hamar, to offer his condolences, the young sultan was urged to be suspicious.

Even though it was a sad time, the dignitaries were greeted with a welcome that was befitting their royal presence. They all stayed in the sultan's palace, and none of the servants they brought with them had to do anything. The sultanate saw to it that their every need was met.

Sultan Ahmed was tall and displayed his wealth in his body weight and in the things he wore. He was a proud man and frequently reminded his audiences that he descended from royalty. No one could beat him in verse competitions in poetry and in Qur'anic memorization. And when he talked, which was often, his deep and loud voice overpowered anything else in the vicinity.

"Today I'm without words," he said, as he brought the young sultan to his chest. "Today you have graduated from my nephew and into my colleague," he added, with the saddest tone anyone had ever heard from him. "I shall treat you with all the respect you deserve."

The young Farah wanted to cry, he so much wanted to relieve his pain, and to grieve for his father. But, he knew, he could not do that in the presence of his enemy.

"Thank you, Sultan Ahmed," he said, addressing the man for the first time in anything other than 'uncle.'

Many others attended the funeral, although none as pronounced as Sultan

Ahmed. Sultans from the West and South also came. And when, in the middle of lunchtime, the afternoon winds rattled the funeral tents, everyone laughed; they knew the Sultan of the Sea had arrived.

After immersing themselves in lamb and aromatic rice, rare vegetables and fruits, the rulers went into one tent to talk, leaving their subjects wondering what they would be discussing.

Before they started their discussion, a eunuch had come into the room and brought to the men the after meal delicacies. A silver plate was placed between them, containing sweet spice mix, areca nuts, and betel leaves.

One by one, as they enjoyed the mind-altering dessert, they offered to secure the sultanate while the young sultan would be on Hajj, extending his father the gift of completing one of his dreams.

The young sultan kindly turned them all down, saying the sultanate would remain in its own care with Bashi, who had now become the Crown Prince himself.

"Can you really trust your uncle?" asked Sultan Gaaboow, who had been the sultan of the neighboring sultanate in the south for over fifty years. "Wasn't it the Crown Prince of Biyoole," he reminded everyone, "Who dethroned his own brother and killed the next one in line?"

The young sultan was not bothered by tales he had grown up with. Instead, with a smile, he said, "I think we all know Bashi had been a better sultan than our people have ever seen," he added, as he looked over to a painting on the wall. "My grandfather only chose my father to keep the peace," he turned back to them, "And I always thought that was a mistake."

The men were horrified.

Hanad could have easily read another chapter, but he didn't want to once he noticed the title of the next chapter was "Journey," which meant it would be a whole new part of the novel. He was too tired.

"Tomorrow," he said to himself.

He closed the book.

But Hanad couldn't sleep.

It was a little after midnight when he sneaked out of his house, walked through the neighborhood, and ended up on Warshaddaha Road. This commercial street was empty at night, as there were hardly any homes on it. It was the perfect place to take a long walk, to clear your mind, to rejuvenate. It was something introduced to him by Ayanle. Whenever they would hang out, they would often end up there late at night. The young Hanad would look up and see the stars.

"They're so bright here," he would say.

Now he could look up on his own. He was not a kid anymore. The stars were still there and brighter than ever.

Then, just like that, a car pulled up.

"Hi," said the driver, as he pulled down the window.

"Hi," replied Hanad.

"Where are you going?"

"Just walking around."

"Do you mind if I walk with you?"

"No," said Hanad, "It's fine."

The man parked the car off the road. When he came out Hanad could see he was a heavyset man. He was older, maybe a bit older than Ayanle but he showed all his years. Hanad knew he could outrun him, so he felt a lot more comfortable.

They walked together.

"I'm Kusow, by the way," said the man, pointing out the belly that inspired his nickname. "What's your name?"

"Hanad."

"You're a beautiful boy, Hanad."

"Thank you," smiled Hanad, "You're very kind."

Of course, Hanad knew exactly what Kusow wanted. Both of them were cosmopolitan. They didn't have to let things get ugly. Kusow didn't push the issue, only hinting at the desire to bed the young man, and Hanad didn't have to reject him for there was no direct offer to reject. Instead, after walking for about half an hour, when Hanad said he was going back to his house, Kusow wanted to exchange phone numbers. Hanad had already felt very comfortable with Kusow by then, and he agreed.

"I will drop you off," said Kusow.

"I can walk, it's no issue."

"It's not negotiable," smiled Kusow.

Hanad was grateful he didn't have to walk back, as they had actually walked a lot further than he had originally intended. Kusow's car wasn't as bad as he expected. It was a lot fresher and less cluttered than he imagined a fat dude's car would be like.

"You have a mobile phone," said Hanad, as he noticed the huge thing between the gearshift and the radio board.

"Actually," chuckled Kusow, "I got it off of my cousin's Corvette. It doesn't go with this Corolla, but I don't care," he laughed. "He is in Russia, studying, and took the keys with him, the fucker."

"So, you stole it," Hanad rolled his eyes.

"I wouldn't say that," smiled Kusow.

"How would you put it?"

"I'm keeping it warm for him."

Hanad laughed.

"This thing cost a $1,000!" laughed Kusow.

"Why pay so much when you can just use the home phone," said Hanad, not getting the whole fuss about mobile phones. "I would rather spend that kind of money to travel."

Hanad got dropped off.

They said good night.

Back in his own bed, as he tossed and turned, Hanad's thoughts were haunting him. These thoughts were equally divided between Farah and Ayanle.

Of course, he didn't want Ayanle in bed, next to him, to help him fall sleep. No, he was worried about him and Bilan. He wondered what happened. Something must have happened; he knew that much.

What happened? Hanad asked himself.

CHAPTER 9

Bilan collected her belongings from work. She gathered her thoughts and emotions, and she got out of that building with little fuss. She left as casually as she had done the day before, and she made no mention of this being her last day. There were no goodbyes, no parties to part ways with her colleagues, and she did not dwell on any of this in her mind. She didn't want to leave, but a pregnant woman had very few choices, and Ayanle had crossed one off the list.

Once she got out of the building, she turned around. There it was. That beautiful sign she adored. *Warshada Sigaarka iyo Taraqa.* She remembered the first time she had seen the thing. She remembered how she had thought the words "matches" and "cigarettes" had never looked so good.

"That is all they manufacture?" she had asked her friend.

"That is more than enough!" her friend had laughed.

Bilan was here once again, and part of her adored the sign as much as she did that first time she had seen it. She felt the same emotions. She felt the same respect for the sign maker, the artist whom she would meet months after she started working at the factory.

At the same time, part of her also felt incredibly sad. She knew a part of her heart was left behind. In that factory, in that building, and in that body of Ayanle. Thinking of the man she loves only makes her tear up. She didn't have to think about what had happened. She didn't have to think about all the awful things he had said to her in that week. She didn't have to think about all the many nights she had spent wondering where he was, with whom he was, and what he was doing.

No, none of that was necessary.

The sign was plenty enough.

"I know him," she remembered Ayanle saying at the time, the first time she had seen it. "I mean, the artist who made the sign for the Howlwadaag District."

"How do you know him?"

"Because I'm a manager here," smiled Ayanle.

So, she wasn't sure if the sign was vital because it was beautiful or because of the story she shared with Ayanle.

It wasn't important anymore.

Nothing was.

Instead, Bilan got into the waiting taxi. Abdi was her normal driver. He had been waiting for thirty minutes, but he didn't make any fuss because she was good for it. She didn't go far and she paid generously. He loved driving her. Her positive attitude toward the world made him hopeful about his future. It didn't hurt that she was beautiful either.

They pulled up in front of her house. "I'll just be a few minutes." Abdi nodded, but still got out to smoke. She always took a while. Suddenly, he felt eyes on him. He looked around the street. He noticed the kids playing nearby. They stopped and were discreetly looking over to where he was. There were women staring. They were standing outside a colorful door. It was a cobalt blue door with some deep orange ends. There were also a few young men, sitting on the steps of another house. Of course, he also noticed the older lady who was in the white window on the second floor of another nearby home.

Everyone was looking at him, the taxi, and the front door that Bilan had been in too much of a hurry to close all the way.

"What is going on?" he asked himself.

Inside, another drama was unfolding. Bilan had already packed, and her bags were waiting, but she couldn't bring herself to leave. She sat on the edge of her bed and looked around her room. She grew up in this house, and she spent many years in this room. It was here that she first learned about love, gossiping with Mulki, her best friend.

"My aunt is in love with her Italian boyfriend!" said Mulki one day, as the girls sat on this very bed. "My mom says they had been sneaking around. Grandma yelled at aunty."

"Really?" laughed Bilan.

They were six and seven. The little girls had no idea what love was. They just knew to be in love equaled to sneaking around, to coming home late at night, to getting yelled at by the elders.

But it was when they were ten and eleven that they understood it could lead to getting married. It was when Mulki's aunt got married to her Italian boyfriend, who ended up converting to the faith for her.

Suddenly, to these little girls, love became a ticket. It was a ticket to get away from their *reer baadiye* parents—people raised in the wild and who had no idea how to relate to their modern world. From Mulki's aunt, the girls learned that love could be a ticket all the way to Rome.

Bilan's tears, sitting on the edge of that bed as a grown woman, were as much about her lost innocence as it were about leaving her room, her home, and her city.

She didn't like being a grownup one bit.

Abdi, on the other hand, grew up in Jowhar. His parents were destitute. He lived on the farm of his parent's employers. He grew up with the cruel jokes of their children, knowing he could never fight back. In Mogadishu, his luck turned around, as he got into driving and became good at it. He loved how it felt to drive, with the wind on his face while he would listen to music. He preferred the times between riders when he had his taxicab all to himself.

Today had its own unique pleasures. He was driving Bilan. Normally that was even better than driving alone. Abdi loved how his heart would race a mile a minute when she sat in the back. She would have her hair parted, each half resting over each breast. She always wore a colorful *dirac*, the French chiffon kaftans Somali women love, which was always so thin you could see through it. Abdi would steal moments and peak through to her bra. He loved how her perfume stayed in his taxicab long after she exited.

Today was different, however. He knew this was a different ride with her. It wasn't just the unusual number of bags he carried to the trunk for her that made him wary. It would probably be their last ride together, if he relied on the gloom in her eyes. Sure, he had taken her before to the airport. He had also picked her up from there. But, somehow, he knew this was going to be different. He didn't dare ask, he was just the driver, but Abdi felt that he would probably never see her again.

"How much time do we have before your flight?"

The question interrupted her thoughts.

"What?"

"When is your flight?" Abdi asked.

"Oh, it is several hours from now," replied Bilan. "I just want to get to the airport early, but there is no rush."

Bilan noticed the concealed sadness in his eyes. It occurred to her that he might have seen more than she would have liked to show. She reasoned with herself that she owed him a better goodbye. After all, she knew that he had taken care of her movements for so long and he was never late. She managed a smile and said, "Would you mind if we took a little drive?"

"Not at all," he instinctively sat up.

Abdi knew what it meant to take a "little drive" with Bilan. She had done this whenever she was down. Suddenly, the request threw him off, and he no longer knew for sure if he was right about the possibility of this particular ride being their last. Was she just sad? Or was there really something more sinister going on?

They drove on Howlwadaag Avenue until they reached Baar Ubax, her favorite restaurant. She made him stop for a second, and the uncontrollable tears on her face let him know he was probably not wrong. She had never done that before, ever. She pulled the window down and took a photo. She remembered all the evenings she spent there, all the dinners with her friends, and she just didn't want to ever forget.

Abdi asked her if she wanted to go inside, but she told him to continue driving.

"Okay," he smiled.

He made a left turn on Thirtieth Road, at the corner from the restaurant. They passed Carwo Idko, the mall in which she often shopped. She wanted to stop at Suuq Bacaad, the market in which her best friend Mulki owned a shop. She wanted to go in there and see her one last time.

But she couldn't.

"No, keep going," she said.

They drove on Janaraal Daa'uud Avenue until they reached Siinaay Road. It was then that Abdi asked if she would prefer to make right and go towards Kaaraan District, where her younger sister was a newlywed. Bilan didn't have to think twice about saying no. So, they continued towards Liido, her favorite beach.

As they drove, Bilan made Abdi stop several times because there were so many memories. There was the little house where Mulki's family lived in for about six months. It was where she lost her virginity.

"Will you love me forever?" she had asked Dahir, who at sixteen had been only two years older than she was.

"Of course," he smiled.

She hadn't needed much else. She had opened her legs, and held onto Dahir for dear life, as he tore through her sown flesh. It was the third most painful moment of her life. The most painful moments were getting sewn up in the first place, and going to the lady who gave her the virginity back. Of course, Mamo Batulo didn't bother to tell her that virginities were something one could never really get back. Instead, she took the teenager's money and put her through yet another zip-up of the worst kind. It got infected and had to be opened once more a few weeks later.

Bilan was most emotional, however, at Liido Beach. Abdi knew this was going to be the most painful stop. He had brought her to the beach so many times. He would wait for her while she was with her friends, soaking up the sun, or simply rejuvenating from long nights. So, of course, Abdi expected the worst. He watched her walk to the water. She got her feet wet, and Abdi could see from a distance that she was crying uncontrollably. Her body shook, and it looked from the back as if her head was getting buried in her chest and the arms were struggling to pull it back. He wanted to go to her, hug her, and tell her he loved her. He wanted to ask her to stay, to let him take care of her, and to make whatever she was running from to go away. He yearned to protect her and give her the type of love he knew Ayanle was never going to give her.

But, alas, he stood there powerless.

The drive from Liido Beach to the airport was long and silent. Bilan mostly looked out the window as if en route to her execution. Abdi periodically stole glimpses through the rearview mirror. They drove through Xamar Wayne, Xamar Jajab, and Waaberi districts, and finally reached the airport through Garoonka Diyaaradaha Avenue.

"Have a safe trip, and I will see you soon," said Abdi, once he loaded her luggage on the cart and sent her way into the airport.

Bilan could not even look at his face, let alone say anything, as she was afraid she would humiliate herself even more. She left far more than what the ride cost in the back of the seat, as she usually did. However, this time, there was a thank you note.

Abdi pulled off the road right outside of the airport and wept.

Bilan walked into the Airbus A310. She sat down, and that is when she noticed the famous slogan, "The White Star Service." It immediately brought her back to the year before when she was traveling with Ayanle. It was a time when she had been happy, when she thought everything in her world was going right, and when she thought he loved her.

"Nonsense," he had smiled, "Their service sucks."

Bilan had hushed him, "It's our national airline. Don't say such things."

"But it's the truth," he had whispered. "They're awful."

They had agreed to disagree.

And now, many months later, she sat here remembering a fight between a proud national and her dissident lover. She wished so much to forget about everything. She wished she could be one of those people she read about in the news, waking up without their memories. Instead, everything reminded her of him.

Dadna waa ismoodoo ... inaan kugu dul meero ... ku dibjiro agtaaddee ... Dadnimadda aqoonso ... jacaylkaan la diiday ... waa intuu ku daarree ... ma ii diir naxaysaa ...

The sad story of a woman, who was rejected by the man she loves, was a bit too close to home for Bilan. No amount of Magool's gracious voice could make her bear it.

"Oh, God," Bilan murmured.

She opened the magazine as the plane shot into the air. The cover was a petite woman on some island. She looked young and happy, and as though there was nothing in this world that could disturb her. Bilan caught herself wishing to be that woman. She wanted to get away from everything she knew so much.

The farther the plane got from her home city the more anxious Bilan became. She dreaded having to go to her big sister. She hated that she would be forced to stay there for months. She worried that she would be giving birth far from her mother. She despised that she was going to give birth without the child's father. She detested that she had turned into her mother.

CHAPTER 10

Kusow drove up to his friend's house. Predictably there was no one waiting. He laid on the horn. Dahir threw a shirt on and popped his head onto the street.

"Two minutes," he pleaded.

"Come on, man!" fired Kusow. "Why?"

"Please," smiled Dahir and went back in.

Dahir continued getting ready. He threw his hair into a frenzy with his new gel. He put some cologne on his cheeks and neck. The gold chain went on last.

In the meantime, Kusow thought about that phone conversation he has had with Hanad earlier that day. He didn't understand what the young man meant by it was the wrong timing. It wasn't exactly the right time to have run into him on the Warshaddaha Road either. At the time he was too caught up to hear him, but now he had time to think about it. He realized the young man was being nice about it but that he was probably in a serious relationship with someone.

"But he's so young," Kusow said to himself. He noticed his friend Dahir was running up to the car. "Let's go!"

Dahir got into the car and Kusow drove off.

"What's that new smell?" asked Kusow.

"Here," Dahir brought his face closer to Kusow's face. "'Proraso' it's called," he told his friend, as he took his body back to its normal position, "She got it for me from Italy. You like?"

"Nice girlfriend," chuckled Kusow.

Kusow drove his ocean blue 1987 Corolla down on Via Sanca, and soon they were parking in front of several small shops crowded together by history. One with red exteriors that thinly separated from its deep orange door was a café. The friends walked into the place, but it didn't seem like anyone was there.

Saredo, the owner, was known to wander through the neighborhood when it was slow. However, at early evening she should have been expecting company. Usually, the place would have been busy by now.

"Sareeeeeedo," yelled out Dahir, knowing she hated when he stretched her name longer than it was meant to be pronounced. "Where are you, dear?"

The boys called out a couple of times, and no one responded. So, they sat down at a table and waited. They had done this many times. Dahir traced his index finger on the table, noticing it was not the cleanest. He had given up asking Saredo to clean the place.

"Why, are you important?" she would bark back confidently.

Saredo was older but sexy. She was in her forties, but she never had children. So, to the boys, she looked "together." She loved wearing the traditional *guntiino* dress, as she liked the way the cotton material wrapped around her body before it was tied over one shoulder. Because she wasn't married, she didn't wear the *shaash* on her head. However, as she was a woman of a certain age, she would wear the *ilyar*, which made her hair breathe out. She never wore *garbisaar*, as she hated the shawls covering her beautiful shoulders. When she walked towards the boys they enjoyed how her braless breasts slowly swayed left and right in her *guntiino*. And, of course, they loved how her butt cheeks did the same when she walked away from them.

"Stop looking at me!" she would protest.

Dahir could almost hear her in his head then, as he sat alone with Kusow there. He shook his head and looked at his friend. It was then that Dahir began to wonder what it was on Kusow's face. There was something he wanted to say, but it seemed like Kusow was hesitating.

"What's up? Talk to me."

"Have you heard about Bilan?"

"What about her?" asked Dahir.

Kusow gave a nervous smile. He always had that on his face whenever he had something to hide. Dahir knew this smile too well.

"Come off with it," said Dahir, bracing himself.

"She left town. No one knows where she went. The rumor is," explained Kusow, "she got pregnant with Ayanle's baby, and he didn't want to marry just yet. She escaped, it is said, to avoid shame."

"Shit!" murmured Dahir.

Kusow knew immediately that Dahir went the direction he feared his friend would. Dahir's face let Kusow know that his friend was blaming it all on himself.

"I knew something bad would happen," said Dahir. "That lowlife Ayanle has no appreciation for life," he added, upset. "I should've—"

"It is not your fault," said Kusow. "She made that choice a long time ago on her own. We all warned her about him. There was no one in this great city who ever thought he was good for her, but what can you do? The heart goes wherever it wants to go."

Then Dahir got up, and his friend Kusow could see he was uncomfortable.

He let him be.

Kusow wondered if it was indeed a good idea to have told Dahir that the love of his life was destroying her life.

Dahir went outside and sat on the trunk of the car. He got lost in his thoughts. He tried to remember the first time he had seen Bilan. They were probably five and seven. It was a long time ago, but the emotions he felt were as present as if they were happening at that moment for the first time. It was just after Islamic school, and he had been busy trying to memorize those Qur'anic verses. She had appeared with her friends. Even now he could feel the strange sensation rise in him as he recalled following her with eyes full of awe. She was the most beautiful thing he had ever seen.

"Can we be friends?" he had asked her weeks later.

"Sure," she had smiled, "Why not?"

Dahir tried to trace his association with Bilan, and he tried his best to recall precisely where things went wrong. Was it when they were ten and twelve when he had kissed her on the lips for the first time? But she had said she loved it. Was it when he made love to her for the first time as teenagers? But he clearly recalled her enjoying it.

"No," he shook his head, so quietly.

No, it was that afternoon, the moment he had introduced her to his old friend Ayanle. He hated that moment. He had seen a new kind of desire in her eyes. Her mouth had parted a little and there seemed to have been some sort of a sigh. He knew it was too late for them, but he had pretended not to know. He pretended not to have noticed what had taken place before his eyes.

Here he was, a few years later, and he learned he had been right all along. He knew what he had known on that fateful afternoon was right. Ayanle would break both their hearts.

"It is okay," he had told her when she came to break up with him weeks after he had introduced them.

Somehow, he knew he should have fought for her. He had felt the instinct to protect her, but he worried she would never forgive him.

Now it was too late.

Kusow had given his friend a respectable time to come to terms with what he had told him. Now it was nearly an hour later, and he knew they would need to get moving if they were going to see that play.

"Are you okay?"

"Yeah," replied Dahir. "Do you mind if we don't go to that play tonight? I'm just not—"

"Of course, it is no problem."

"Thank you," he tried to smile.

That evening the friends went to Liido Beach, instead. They sat there in the dark, listening to the sad songs beaming from the beach hotels.

Ha'i oranin... iska tag... ha imaan ...

This song was sung by Qasin Hilowle, in a sad love story where his lover kept pushing him away. The singer was well known for romantic songs. He knew how to emphasize different parts of the song. His voice nearly whispered "don't tell me," only to rise as he sang "go away," before dropping again, with a weak "and don't come back."

The song made Dahir think about that a day years earlier—once again—when Bilan had came to him to break it off. Part of him wished he had said those lines. Part of him wondered if she would have stayed had she heard his voice, like Qasin, breaking down and rising and coming back down again. He wondered if the romantic melodies of down and up and down again would convey the mighty reasoning of his heart. He wondered what would have happened if he had said that life is about ups and downs, and if you stick to it everything will be beautiful in the end—just like a piece of music.

Instead, he closed his eyes and remembered her. Bilan's almond-shaped eyes were deep brown, and they were eyes that were utterly confident in what they were, what they saw, and what they wanted.

"Your eyes always speak to me as the fire speaks to the strongest of the insects," he had once told her, as they lay on the sand under a sky colored deep orange by the setting sun.

"What does the fire say to the insects?"

He had chuckled, and replied, "I love you."

Bilan had laughed.

"Mean fire, I know," he had joined her in laughter.

But it wasn't just the eyes that attracted and burned Dahir. It was also her lips. He had never seen lips as perfectly placed as hers. The eyes might have delighted his heart, as they surely did, but it was her lips that made him stay in the fire. It was undoubtedly the lips that made him feel all his atoms breaking down in the high heat of her emotional being.

Then, of course, there was her nose—a pillar that kept the structure all together. It jumped between the eyes, and yet it curved immediately after in a decline that resisted falling until the lips kept it at bay. Dahir loved placing his finger between her eyes and following the magnificent journey that was her nose.

But what is a structure without a base? Bilan's cheekbones, lovely and strong, were the real place where he felt most at home. The nose might have sprung out of the eyes, and the lips might have had their battles to keep the nose from leaping out of her face, but it was the cheekbones that made everything stay together in harmony. Dahir loved the way they felt against his, as he felt the soft and feminine nature of her spirit.

Ha'i oranin… iska tag… ha imaan …

Dahir was snatched back to the sad present moment. He wished he could return to that moment when he was living for her face. He wished he was a teenager again, admiring the beauty that was forming before his very eyes.

That night, the young men stayed at the beach until dawn. There was many a time when Kusow sleepily thought they should leave. Yet, he couldn't bring himself to say the words. He knew his friend needed the time to heal. He thought that giving Dahir this time was the only way he could contribute to his healing. He knew if Dahir went home he wouldn't be afforded the luxury of disappearing into the sounds of the ocean. The snores of his family would have interrupted his needs.

"Man, my dad snores like crazy," he had once laughed with Kusow. "We can all hear it from every room!"

"Damn, at least you don't have to worry about thieves coming." Kusow had laughed. "That man is keeping you all safe with that snoring!"

"But, Bro, we are dying!" he had laughed with him.

No, home would not have been the best place to process all of what was happening.

He gave his friend what he needed.

CHAPTER 11

It was a little after sunrise when Kusow arrived in front of Hanad's house. He parked, got out of the car, and went around the house. He found Hanad's room in the back of the house. Kusow knew it was Hanad's because he has said on the phone the day before that there is an Italian flag on his window. It was another reason to love Hanad, as this rebellious act could have gotten him arrested or worse. Kusow looked around and picked up a few small stones. He threw them at the window, one by one. It took seven of them to get Hanad to wake up.

"Man, what are you doing?"

"Hi, beautiful," smiled Kusow.

"Sheesh! You're crazy! Everyone is sleeping."

"So, I still feel fresh for you!"

Hanad smiled, shook his head, and closed the window. A minute later he was outside, talking to Kusow. "Why are you up so early?"

"I had to help a friend, so I never got to bed. He lives on your street."

"That explains it," chuckled Hanad.

"What?"

"I never took you as the morning type."

"No, I'm not," laughed Kusow.

"Go home and sleep," smiled Hanad. "I have to get back and try to sleep for an hour before I actually have to get up," he turned back to his house, and then turned around, "But, please, don't make this a thing. I don't—"

"Just wanted to be spontaneous."

"That you are!"

Kusow blew him a kiss.

Hanad shook his head.

Back in his room Hanad found it difficult to go back sleep. He tried for a few minutes, but he was definitely too awake for that to ever happen. Instead, he took out his novel and read…

Journey

The boy who was a sultan woke up about an hour before dawn. It was the day of his journey. He had planned to leave the eighth of Shawwal when the moon was half full. This period was chosen so that the moon could always be a companion over his fifteen-night sailing to Zayla.

He would spend a few days in Zayla and then head to Aden, which would take another four days.

From Aden, which was one of the cities on the route that he had actually been looking forward to visiting, he would go with a caravan to reach Mecca and offer his pilgrimage.

The young Sultan would be traveling on a somewhat new dhow, which had been purchased in Zanj the year before. The lateen-rigged vessel was named after a queen of Zanj, Nimobwe, and came with two masts.

When it arrived in Hamar, after two tumultuous days in the Indian Ocean, Sultan Aweys had its name changed upon seeing it. She was named after Araweelo, a queen of the Somali.

Now, Araweelo would carry its new Sultan as part of his holy trip to the pilgrimage.

"I wish it could take you to Mecca itself," lamented Bashi, "But you want adventure, so…"

The young sultan was adamant that no royal family members accompany him. He also did not want Warsame, his favorite wazir, to come along.

It was soon going to be the *jilal*, the driest of the seasons, and wanted everyone who was important to be home. So, the young sultan only wanted to take with him the crew, most of whom the young sultan never even met.

I need to experience this for myself, he reasoned, if I make it on my own, then no one can ever take it away from me. It will be my own success.

After breakfast, the young sultan was given a royal sendoff. He insisted on walking from his palace to the harbor. Bashi, the wazirs, and the amirs walked behind him, while a silk canopy was held above the sultan's head, to protect him from the morning sun. The best entertainers, the dancers, and the musicians walked ahead of them, while his subjects filled both sides of the road.

The young sultan waved to everyone, some seeing him for the first time in their lives, and others were known to him all his life.

Some of the people had tears in their eyes, while many others watched in awe.

Part of him wondered if he would survive his trip. In case he did not, he knew there was a letter with Bashi, detailing all of his affairs.

At the harbor the dhow, Araweelo, was ready. The sultan saw she was decorated with all sorts of colorful items, some of which he recognized from personal items his mother must have given. There was a blanket from his infancy age, which he adored as a child.

"Get rid of that," he directed one of the wazirs, who immediately removed the blanket.

The sultan was a man now. He did not need to be reminded of his childhood.

Mid-morning the dhow sailed into the horizon. If all went well, they would arrive in Zayla about two weeks later. It was the perfect time to travel, as the monsoon had already left, and now the ocean was calmer.

To occupy his time, the sultan would read. He finally had the chance to read al-Tabari, something his father had made him promise he would do as soon as he could.

The History of the Prophets and Kings was precisely what he needed. These volumes were filled with stories of people important to him, to his people, and to his faith. He would neither get bored with them nor would he tire of delving into their lives.

When he was not reading, the young sultan spent his time gazing into the horizon, thinking about his family, and the well being of his people.

He spent many hours reading the Qur'an, praying, and meditating.

His soul was preparing for the pilgrimage.

Hanad really liked this story and continued reading…

Sultanate of Ifat

The evening view of Zayla in the distance was marvelous. The lamps illuminating from the homes complimented the big light on the sky. It all looked glorious. Here was the last stop before reaching Arabia.

As they got closer and closer to the harbor, the sultan could see two of his wazirs waving and with smiling faces. They had arrived three days before him, to prepare for a smooth stay, and now they were happy their sultan had come safely.

The young sultan's wazirs were accompanied by local wazirs, who were as welcoming as they had been to his father the year before.

"Unfortunately," said one of the local wazirs, "Our sultan is away, as he is attending the wedding celebrations of a neighboring sultan," added the man, with promises to take care of all the needs of the sultan.

The capital of the Sultanate of Ifat was everything the young sultan had heard all his life. It was full of different faces, with a population that spoke different languages, and was booming with business.

Over a state dinner, the traveling sultan was introduced to key individuals in the sultanate and was entertained with local flavors in food and music.

It was then that his nose detected something new. A fragrance he had never smelt before. He looked up, and around him, and there she was.

She was slim, tall, and all the things that generally did not grab his attention. She had skin as fair as the girls his father had wanted him to marry, and he wanted something different. He liked his women meaty, much shorter, and darker.

He knew, if there were no protest, he would have liked to marry a woman from the Gikuyu tribe. He had seen them few years before when he traveled with his father to their land, to visit the famed mountain of Kirinyaga.

Another person walked into the room. This time it was a man. He was taller, and his shoulders were broad, his face long, and had the most beautiful eyes the young sultan had ever seen.

The stranger was wrapped in orange fabric, and when he walked passed him the sultan knew it was the person he scented. He got a stronger whiff of that fragrance.

He was instantly struck with deep feelings for a man he had never met before. He was a bit taken back by his own reaction and felt a little embarrassed because he did not even see his face entirely.

"Who is that man?"

"He is a Mandinka prince," said a local wazir, as that prince sat down on the other side of the long table, "he belongs to an ethnic group in the Mali Empire," he added when he realized the young sultan didn't know.

"Ah," he smiled at him.

The prince nodded.

Throughout dinner and dessert, as different people from different royal backgrounds talked about their lives and adventures, the young sultan was smitten with the prince, looking at his direction as often as he could.

The more time passed, the more the young sultan could not shake the feelings of desire off his mind and body. He was physically and psychologically in trouble, and he knew he had better watch it.

Yet, there was something diabolically sweet about it all. The young sultan enjoyed being a bad boy, desiring strangers, and being physically trapped in his seat.

May Allah forgive me, he thought.

Now the story was getting interesting. It was impossible to put it down. So, of course, he continued reading...

Prince Bilal

After dinner, a wazir had arranged a private meeting on the terrace, between the prince and Sultan Farah. They spoke Arabic, even though the prince had a different *lahjah*, a dialect he wasn't familiar with.

Nevertheless, he loved the way he sounded.

The two spent several minutes conversing. The prince immediately admitted he knew who the young sultan was.

"You were announced the previous night over dinner," he smiled.

As the prince spoke, the young sultan was feeling stronger and stronger about him, and it was beginning to irk him.

I can control my desires, he thought, even if he is the most beautiful being I had ever seen.

The prince's name was Bilal, and he was aged nineteen. He had been on the road since the year before when he had taken his mother to the pilgrimage.

"You could say I had always known I would be the one to take her," he said, as they looked into the distance, towards the harbor and the sea beyond. "I must have been ten or so," he added, as he looked over to the sultan, admiringly, "It was my older brother who informed me. 'I would have been the one,' he told me, 'But you came and now it will be your responsibility.'"

Prince Bilal said he was never one to refuse a challenge, and on his seventeenth year of life, he and his mother had gotten on the road to the pilgrimage.

Afterward, said the prince, they visited various countries on the Arabian Peninsula before his mother had succumbed to a deadly snakebite in Salalah.

"I'm very sorry," the young sultan had said, as he placed his right hand over his own heart, "I'm sorry to hear about your mother. From God we come, and to Him we return," he added, now placing that hand on the shoulder of the prince, "God willing, you will be reunited one day."

"Thank you," smiled the prince, "*Insha Allah.*"

For a moment neither of them had said anything else, and both of them could feel that something was going on, although neither of them dared to ask.

"I'm going to the pilgrimage myself," said the young sultan, without telling him it was for his late father."

The prince nodded, "May God accept your effort."

The sultan wanted to tell his new friend about his father, but he feared he might be seen in a negative light; as though he was competing with the prince's loss.

So, instead, he smiled and said, "Thank you."

"What is your sultanate like?"

"Oh, it's very nice," said the young sultan, "It's bigger than our neighbors', and I would say it's probably double the size of this one."

"That is quite big," smiled the prince.

"Indeed. Of course, not as big as your empire."

"Yes," chuckled the prince, "Not as big."

"What's the population there these days?"

"I think we reached a good two million strong."

"That's impressive!"

"Yes," smiled the prince.

Despite their try at lightening the conversation, the two of them knew there was something more serious brewing in the air.

The handsome prince took a deep breath, and the sultan exhaled—and neither of them could deny that they had become so intimate that they could hear each other's breathing.

They agreed to go to the beach together.

Hanad looked over at the clock on his wall and he knew he had enough time to read a few more chapters. Even though for a moment, he wondered if he should do it, he eventually dived in…

Bilal

The breeze on the beach was exactly what they needed. It was so fresh, and the closer they got to the water the more that stinking fish in the air disappeared. Zayla was a beautiful place, full of culture and diversity, but it was always stinking of fish, thought the young sultan.

Prince Bilal, who had been staying for some days before the young sultan had arrived, agreed with him.

The young sultan chuckled, "But the fish is good!"

As they laughed, the backs of their hands brushed against one another; and they naturally held hands.

"I want to confess something," said Bilal.

"Tell me," Farah got closer, as they walked.

"When you arrived, I saw you. I was in my room, which faces the harbor, and I saw the wazirs bring you and…" then he hesitated for a moment.

"And?"

"And I wanted to come down and greet you."

"Only greet?"

The prince smiled, "I wanted to touch you."

"Like now," Farah held up their hands together; still the fingers intertwined.

"I suppose so," chuckled the prince.

Once they were in front of the sea, neither one of them spoke for a moment.

"My father died recently," said the young sultan.

"Oh," Bilal squeezed the sultan's hand, "I'm sorry," he said, as he turned to hug, "I'm very sorry."

Then the young sultan felt something he had not explored all along. He felt a strong sense of pain. It was physical pain, but he thought it was all sitting in his chest.

Intuitively the prince kissed the neck of the sultan.

Then the young sultan broke into a sobbing fit.

Soon, the prince was also sobbing.

They sobbed together for a while, each feeling the loss of their parent. They felt safe with one another. Neither of them needed to be a royal person. They were only human beings. They were young men grieving for their loved ones, whom they could no longer see in the physical world.

After they finished, they realized they both wet the other's garment with their tears.

"I didn't have a chance to cry," said the prince.

"I know what you mean," agreed his new friend.

Now they could sit and talk. And talk they did. The two talked about their lives. Bilal told Farah about the Mali Empire, and Farah told him about the Sultanate of Mogadishu. They were only sharing information, neither of them felt jealous of the other's land.

Then the topic of conversation veered into the personal, and soon they were onto their sexual histories. Farah was the first one to admit he liked men and women equally. Bilal said he liked the men more, and if forced he could find interest in women.

Back home, Farah said, he was in love with his wazir. He told him all about Warsame and their history. He said he was devastated when Warsame married. He said, before that moment, he had been confident they were going to be together forever.

But, he also talked about a girl named Jawhara. She was the beautiful daughter of a man who traded spices. After Warsame married, he was going to marry Jawhara, but his father did not allow it.

The more Farah talked about Jawhara, the less Bilal seemed to be interested in anything anymore.

Then, suddenly, Bilal got up, "I'm sleepy."

"Oh," said Farah, joining him.

"I'm sorry," said the prince.

"No, we have all had a long day."

They walked back to the palace, and each went to his room, although Farah kept his door open just in case Bilal wanted to come to him.

He closed the door after several hours.

Hanad was now absolutely in love with the story. He wondered what it was like to live at that time. He has seen historical movies from European countries, and he had certainly read many novels of the old days, but it felt different to read an ancient story of the same Somali city he was living in. Hanad wondered if he would be as daring as the Farah in the story. He wondered if he would have the courage to go up to someone he desired like that. He wondered if he would even have taken such a risky journey the way the young man to his Islamic pilgrimage had. He smiled, shook his head, and continued reading…

Life with Bilal

The next morning the young sultan woke up much later than he was used to. He did not realize how tired he had been until he woke up; his body felt fresher than it had in days. Unfortunately, he woke up to some bad news. A local wazir informed the young sultan that Bilal had departed early that morning.

He said nothing about him.

He did not leave a note.

He just left.

Sultan Farah was sad for the rest of the day, feeling like a fool. How could he think a traveling man would just return his feelings? But, he thought, he knew there was something there. He felt it.

I must have imagined it, he thought.

Yet, as he went about his day, at different times and at different places, he would get a whiff of his fragrance.

In the afternoon, as a wazir was showing him to the big market, Farah saw a man in the distance. Convinced it was Bilal, he went up to him, stood behind him and it seemed as though he was trying to smell the man's neck.

The wazir had to grab his hand and pull him away before others noticed.

"Did you know that man?" asked the horrified wazir, as the young sultan apologized for his behavior.

"No," he said, a bit embarrassed, "I thought it was someone I knew."

Also, later, as they walked near outskirts of the town, the young sultan heard his prince talking to him. He looked around and found no one.

While he was having dinner, with a room full of people who were looking to him to tell stories of his sultanate, the young sultan was deeply distracted by thoughts of Bilal.

There were so many things running through his mind. He was even daydreaming about the two of them, being together, and traveling together.

There was even a lovely little house on a hill, on an island, in his daydream. There were coconut trees, and the sea was nearby. From every corner of the house, you could see the sea in the distance.

"My sultan," said one of his wazirs, with a worried tone, "Are you alright?"

But the young sultan was stretching himself in a hammock on that island, beside that house, under the coconut trees.

"My sultan," his wazir touched him on the arm.

"Yes," he smiled, back to the reality.

"Would you like to go lie down?"

"No, I'm alright."

However, the young sultan was feeling concerned. He did not understand any of it.

What was all this about?

I did not come here to meet a man, he thought, and I certainly did not come here to fantasize about a fake life; I came here to go to the pilgrimage, and to defend the soul of my father by fulfilling something required of him.

That night, after dinner, when he retired to his room, Sultan Farah was wholly lost in his thoughts. He tried to think about all the things his father had taught him. He remembered one particular conversation in which his father warned him against romantic love.

"Love can make you weak," he told him.

Now he understood what his father was talking about. He felt weak. He was getting terribly distracted and wondered if the people in that house would not report bad behaviors from him.

He prayed to Allah to remove his obstacles. In a day's time, he was planning to go forward to Aden, to Yemen, and did not want to be distracted any longer.

I need to focus, he thought.

Hanad stop his reading here. He realized the next chapter would take the reader away from the story, and he thought it was the perfect place to stop.

CHAPTER 12

"Wake up," said my mother, as she poked me on the shoulder with her index finger, "That young man is on the phone again."

I knew who it was before I opened my eyes.

"Hanad," she murmured to herself, "What kind of a boy's name is that? What type of parents name their son such a thing?"

I could hear her reach the door, and then turn around.

"Who is he, anyway?" she asked.

I got to the phone as quickly as I could, even though I was half sleep and very tired. I hoped Hanad didn't feel my frustration on the other end, as I quickly said to him "Hanad, I will call you back. I was sleeping."

"I haven't seen you in so long."

"I know. I am smiling just from hearing your voice."

"Soon?"

"Soon."

Finally Hanad and I were able to meet alone for the first time. My mom decided to spend the night with Saredo, who has been one of her oldest friends. Saredo had run away from home at age thirteen, hoping to become a singer in the Somali capital. Things didn't work out I guess, because she was now running a coffee shop. She and mom would spend hours together on the phone and once she went to Hargeisa to meet her.

"For a long time, I blamed her for Asli moving to Mogadishu," my mom told me on the plane ride to Mogadishu, "It was because of her that she met that lowlife of a man that your aunt marr—" then mom stopped herself, "I hope God will have Mercy on him, as I hate to speak ill of the dead."

Somewhere along the way mom finally realized Aunt Asli was old enough to make her decisions and that she was responsible for her life. Mom and Saredo had made their way back to each other, and I couldn't have been happier about it for it gave me a chance to meet Hanad at the hotel.

"This is a very nice hotel," said Hanad. We walked around the pool on the roof. "I rarely get a chance to see the city like this," he added, as he looked over to the city.

"I'm happy you like it," I smiled, even though I was feeling anxious.

Hanad walked over to the edge of the roof. Now he could view the city. He was smiling and looked very happy. It was nice to watch Hanad be happy like that. At the same time, I didn't want to waste our time looking at the views. I walked over to him, placed my hands around his waist, and brought my mouth to his ear.

"Can we go to the room now?" I whispered to him.

"No," he chuckled and walked away. "I want to see the gym!"

I shook my head and I followed him into the elevator. I had to keep my hands to myself during the ride, which was really hard, because I was afraid I was going to devour him in the elevator. No one was using the gym, but I was surprised to see they had a Jane Fonda exercise video playing on the TV set.

"I love her," smiled Hanad. "Isn't she amazing?"

I made a gesture of agreement, and then I got closer to him, "Can we please now go?"

"Fine." He was almost resisting, even though I knew he wanted me as much as I wanted him. "Lead the way."

Then he wanted a tour in the hotel room, too! I couldn't believe it. I loudly protested as I began to undress him.

"You're in such hurry," he teased.

I kissed him, as I knew it would shut him up.

Hanad is a great kisser. I love getting kissed by him. He kisses me in ways that no one ever kissed me before. He kisses like he cares, like he is totally in the moment.

"Wait," I interrupted our kissing.

"No, please." He held me closer. His eyes were so full of desire for me that I almost gave in. "Don't stop."

"Two seconds. I promise." I grabbed the boombox and played a song I knew he would like.

He knew it from the very first note of music. He closed his eyes and smiled. Dalida sang "Loin de moi."

L'ennui me gene ... Je n'y peut rien ... Quoi qu'il advienne ... L'ennui me tient ...

He has the most beautiful body I had ever seen. He is slim and yet everything is in the right place. He is really proportionate. Looking at his gentle, round face always makes me smile. The desire in his rounded eyes give me all the approval I ever need in life, but it is his lips, deliciously brown and full, that make me feel weak in my knees. I can't help but see images of what I want to do to them, even if some of these things worry me they will scare him away. What would he do, I asked myself, if I were to ejaculate on them? Would his tongue peak through to lick it off?

I was in his arms again before the answer to that question came from the fearful corners of my imagination. Instead, like a saving grace, he asked a question I could answer.

"Do you like me?" he asked me.

"I like you a lot," I replied without any hesitation. I let my lips creep north on his face and planted a kiss on his forehead. "I like you like I've never liked anyone before." I closed my eyes, as I felt his hands on my back. His hands stopped and caressed the area just before the shoulders meet.

"Good," he said, as he moved his head to the side of my neck. His tongue explored the back of my earlobe—a place no one had ever kissed before—and I moaned.

"Oh, my God," I whispered. My whole body was shaking.

Hanad explored my body and I explored his. Dalida continued to play until the cassette ran out. We were only left with our own music. The understanding came over me that it is the most beautiful music anyone ever wants to hear.

Hours later, Hanad and I woke up. No, Hanad woke me up. He was hungry. It was literally in the middle of the night. I didn't know any place that would be open. I guess, neither of us had this type of experience and we did not realize taking a nap after making love like that could lead to oversleeping. Not that I regretted anything, because I didn't, but I wished I listened to him and gotten some take-away.

"There is some *odkac* in the fridge," I returned to the room and noticed that he was already getting dressed. "You want some?"

"No," he laughed scornfully. "Are we nomads? Why would you want to eat some dried-up old thing like that? I want to go out. Let's go out," he added, "Mogadishu doesn't sleep at night in some parts. We just need to find the right neighborhood."

"Fine." I began to dress.

The front desk guy said nothing nearby would be open, but he did tell us there was a little hole in the wall that was open all night.

It was a thirty-minute walk.

The place was really small and had only two things left on the menu: tea and tea. Somali tea and Indian tea. Black tea or tea with milk. I couldn't believe it.

So, of course, we had tea. It was the best tea I had ever had.

Over the next few weeks, Hanad and I grew closer and closer, and we made love more and more often. We met every night. I would wait until my mother was sleeping, then I would drive over, and pick up Hanad. We would always end up at Liido Beach. We would talk and talk and talk. We would also make love. We would stay until an hour before sunrise.

"I'm very happy," Hanad said once, as I was dropping him off. "I'm very glad I met you."

I smiled.

If you were me, if you were someone like me, someone who was raised in a harsh culture like that of the United Kingdom, where everyone fears you for some reason or another, where the hatred you face for being a black person is only matched by the hatred you face for being a gay person, where no one takes the time to get to know the real you, where everyone assumes you must need something from them if you are there, where the fact that you have as much right as anyone in the country you grew up in is easily overlooked.

If you were someone like that, and you met someone like him; someone who lives in an equally oppressive culture, where someone might hate you simply because you belong to this tribe or that tribe, where people just as easily overlook your right to freedom because you don't have family members in high places.

If you were me and you met someone like him, what would you do?

If you were me, with the type of baggage I carry on my shoulders all the time. If you were a son who was forced to leave his country to accompany his mother to her country, a country you never understood nor taken as yours. If you were someone who was disposable in your family because you're not a husband or a father.

If you were me and you met him, would you want to run away with him like I wanted to at that cafe with only two types of tea?

If you were me, with the type of passport I have, which allows you to go anywhere, and you met someone like him, with a passport that you can't go anywhere with.

If you were me, and if you came from a country like mine, which is a country where everyone respects and wants to do business with, and you met someone like him, someone who comes from a country that everyone is afraid is a bomb that is going to go off any minute.

If you were me and you met someone like him, where would you go?

CHAPTER 13

It had been a few days since Hanad had heard back from Farah. At this point he didn't even hope for a meeting, but he missed Farah's voice. Hanad wondered why Farah was avoiding him. He asked himself if he had done anything wrong, and he couldn't think of anything. There was nothing he could do but wait.

Friday there is no school in that Muslim society. Hanad thought he should spend it at the beach. He went there after a late breakfast and was there until late evening. He swam and played soccer with boys he just met. He was doing everything he could to be physically busy. He spoke to the Italian tourists that were tanning and enjoying the African sun. They enjoyed talking to the smart, well-spoken young man in their own mother tongue.

"This is why I love coming to Somalia," said one man named Marco, who Hanad thought was probably in his early thirties, "So many people speak Italian!"

"But we also enjoy being in 'The White Pearl of the Indian Ocean,' which is a real paradise," countered his lover, Luca, who was a little older. He kissed Marco on the lips, and then turning to Hanad. "Not just because it is easy to travel."

Hanad smiled.

"Of course, I agree," said Marco.

When the sun was not as hot, around four in the afternoon, Hanad decided to read his novel...

Aden

It took four days to reach Aden, and the young sultan finally separated from his crew. They would return to Mogadishu and would arrive there in about three weeks. They would have been away from their families for a month and a half, and they would be happy to be home.

Aden was much more commercial than Zayla, and the young sultan was fascinated with the diversity there. The first person he met was a merchant, a meeting arranged by his wazirs ahead of time.

"Peace be upon you," said a voice behind him, just moments after the young sultan had gotten off the boat, "Are you the Sultan of Mogadishu?"

The merchant had the man at the port, watching out for the young sultan.

The messenger had taken the young sultan through a busy thoroughfare.

The merchant was an Indian man whose parents had migrated to the city from

Calicut. He spoke Arabic with a local accent like any Arab would. The young sultan was treated to a lovely rest, in a beautiful suite overlooking a gorgeous garden.

In the afternoon, after a long sleep, he wandered in the streets of Aden and met many faces.

That is when he saw Bilal. He was talking to a man, and he seemed to be in good spirits. The young sultan approached them, and the closer he got the more he was noticed by the men he was approaching.

Yet, he realized he was not Bilal.

"I'm sorry," he smiled, "I thought you were someone I knew," he added, as the men got back to their conversation.

Even far away, Bilal was haunting him. The young sultan was now wondering if he would ever get rid of him. Perhaps he was of the *jinn*, a demon, and he was sent to distract him from the right thing he had been planning to do.

I will not allow anyone to turn me away from my father, the young sultan thought, as he walked back to the merchant's home.

That evening, the merchant told the young sultan that he would board another ship in two days' time. This ship would stop at several places and finally would reach Jeddah, which was not very far from the holy sites.

As he lay in bed, he was focusing his thoughts on the pilgrimage. He thought if God willed, he would soon be a *haji*, a title he long thought was reserved for old men.

Then, his thoughts drifted to Warsame. He saw the love of his life, in the corner of his third eye, as his eyes closed, and watched him come to the center and laugh.

"You, a haji?" Warsame laughed.

The young sultan loved the familiar feeling of being with Warsame. The way his hands automatically went to his, pulling him closer and closer until he could smell his very breath.

"A Haji who loves you," he smiled.

"But now you're old," taunted Warsame.

Farah laughed and awoke himself with the laughter.

He was sleeping in a comfortable bed, in Aden, many cities away from his lover, and yet he could not keep him in thoughts.

Bilal was back.

He was stronger than ever.

Now he would never sleep, as he wandered through the Indian Ocean in his mind, looking for his prince.

So, he closed his eyes and smiled.

Hanad felt very bad for the Farah in the novel. He identified with him because here he was a thousand years later and he himself was dealing with an African lover who has issues. Why couldn't their African men be as normal about their love as Marco and Luca and the many Europeans he had seen over the years? He was attracted to the beautiful Somali men he had seen growing up in Mogadishu, but he yearned for the ease he saw between European men. Why did Africans allow Arab and European colonialism and religious imperialism make them feel ashamed about who they were? Why couldn't they just be happy with their lovers, without extra issues?

"Oh, why?" asked Hanad, as he looked up to the sky, talking to God.

Although he was not really feeling it Hanad decided to read more…

Haji

The sun was high in the mid-afternoon when the young sultan arrived back to his home city. No one had expected for him to be back so fast, as everyone assumed he would take his time in visiting other countries.

Yet, here he was. He was back within three weeks of the pilgrimage finishing.

Of course, no one questioned his being back. So much had been left undone, waiting for the sultan's approval on this, that, or the other.

"We are happy to have you back," his uncle, Bashi, told him, as they went over all the issues that had arisen while the young Sultan was away.

A celebration was ordered, and a feast was to be had for dinner.

Everyone was invited.

There had been nasty rumors, which began circulating several weeks after the sultan's departure. One of them said he was lost at sea.

"Another one had said," smiled Warsame, "That you were killed in a fishing accident."

"Fishing accident!"

"They don't know you, these people."

"I would never fish!"

Warsame laughed.

Soon, Warsame's face changed more seriously. There was definitely something on his mind. However, before he could say whatever it was he was going to say, Bashi interrupted the young men.

It will have to wait, thought Warsame.

The feast was the largest they had seen in years. So much food was left over after it was finished, and it had to be dispersed amongst the poor on the streets.

It was not a waste, however, as the young sultan took his place and all the nasty rumors had been squashed.

All the members of high society had come, and many of them had approached the young sultan and told them they felt good to know he was very much alive.

But someone was missing from dinner.

"Where is Dahir?" asked the young sultan, wondering why his brother didn't show up.

An uncomfortable silence followed.

"What is going on?"

"A month ago," said Warsame, "Dahir announced he was going to Egypt and left the following day without even saying goodbye to anyone."

"He went to Egypt? Why?"

"We suspect it was a woman," said Bashi.

After dinner, Warsame took the young sultan to the side. He wanted to tell him something before he had heard it from anyone else.

They went to the palace's library.

"What is it?"

"She is pregnant," said Warsame, looking away.

The young sultan wanted to congratulate him, but somehow the words did not come out.

"Since when?"

"I think two months."

A moment of silence followed.

"I met someone," finally the young sultan said.

"You have?"

"Yes, he is—"

"Oh," Warsame was taken aback.

"What?"

"I didn't think it was a man."

"Because you're the only one for me?"

"No, that's not what I meant."

"I'm sorry," said the young sultan, "I know what you meant, but… I guess I'm a little upset," he stood up, and walked to the other side of the room, sitting at the windowsill, "How did we get here? You're married to someone, and I'm meeting others."

"We grew up," said Warsame, joining him, and sitting next to him, "We always knew we would grow up."

"I hate being a grown up."

"You're the sultan," he smiled.

"It doesn't mean anything."

"It means a lot," he reached for the sultan's hand, and when he got a hold of it, he caressed it, "You're so lucky to be a sultan, and you know that."

"I guess," the young sultan looked at the ceiling.

"Who is the man you met?"
"A prince from the Mali Empire."
Neither of them said anything after that.

Hanad closed the book. He couldn't read it anymore. It was too painful. There were just too many reminders from his own young experiences. Instead, he went back to his new Italian friends. They were having coffee and deserts at Café Liido and they were happy to see their friend finally leave the sun and join them.

"Ouch! I'm all sunburnt. You're so lucky you're so dark," said Marco.

"Marco!" said Luca, shocked.

"I know you don't mean anything by it," said Hanad, "But you can't say things like that in Africa. We are not lucky to be dark just like we are not unlucky to be—"

"I'm sorry, I didn't mean to offend," said Marco.

"I know," said Hanad. "I'm just saying, for us our skin, our experiences, our countries—they are all just normal. So, when you make a point about it, keeping in mind the history, we look at you suspiciously."

"I know," said Marco, ashamed. "I'm very sorry. I hope you can see it was an honest mistake."

Hanad knew Marco was not particularly racist but that he was from a system where sensitivities to African peoples are not necessarily kept in mind.

"I just realized something," said Hanad, smiling, as if something marvelous just popped into his pretty brain.

His Italian friends didn't understand.

"This was the first time I didn't think about him."

"About who?" asked Luca.

"Farah," Hanad rolled his eyes. "He is a guy I'm seeing, and he is avoiding me. I haven't heard from him in days and I was feeling a bit obsessive about it."

"You're exactly like Luca!" Marco laughed.

Luca protested. "That is not true!"

"Yes, it is," Marco teased. "Once, I didn't talk to him for a few days because I was traveling with my mother and he wrote me a breakup letter that I found once I returned."

Hanad laughed.

"It wasn't a few days!" Luca turned to Hanad for support. "He didn't say anything to me for three weeks!"

"Why didn't you tell him you were leaving?" The solution seemed obvious to Hanad.

"It was an emergency," Marco protested.

"So, tell us about your friend," said Luca.

"He is really beautiful," Hanad took a photo of the two of them on the beach.

"Oh, he is delicious," said Luca, his eyes fixated on Farah.

"Excuse me?" Marco hit him on the arm.

"Well, he is!" Luca laughed.

"But he is also troubled, I think," Hanad said sadly.

The following evening Hanad went out with his new friends to a party at an Italian man's house. Many people hit on him, both Italian and Somali, but the young Hanad was just not in the mood. He met a lot of people, but it was an Italian/Somali couple that definitely made a memorable impression. Roberto, the Italian, just came over and kissed Hanad on the lips, which literally shook the young man.

"Are you crazy?" Hanad jumped back.

"Oh, it is just love," said smiling Roberto.

For the rest of the night Hanad was held captive by the gazes of Roberto, who desired him openly, and Kamal, the jealous Somali lover, who was afraid Hanad could take his place in the life of his rich man. Of course, Hanad did not want to be with Roberto. He was not interested in being in anyone's life except his Farah. He was just bored to tears with all of these sexual advances.

"We all suffer Roberto," said a young Somali man, who came up to Hanad when he saw what the poor boy was dealing with. "I think you are smart guy. I probably don't have to warn you about these types of people, but Roberto is the worst."

"Is he always like that? Because in Somalia they will kill him if he does that to the wrong person," said Hanad. "By the way, I'm Hanad," he extended his hand to the stranger, smiling.

"Hello, I'm Deeq," said the young man, smiling.

Deeq was exactly what the young Hanad needed at that moment, but he also turned out to be very interesting. He was a writer and was working with a local legend, the man who opened the most important "gay" bar in town. Deeq was writing the man's biography.

"I'm doing it for young people like you and me," said Deeq, smiling, "We need to know our full story. We are not going to expect to find that in government books. They don't want sexual diversity."

"I'm in form four, my last year," said Hanad, "I never learned anything real. I mean, in general."

"Yes, it is unfortunate, but that is the reality of our country," said Deeq, as he sipped his wine, "I think every community needs to work on their own histories."

"I agree completely!" said Hanad. "I was just telling my Italian friends that they need to support Italian-Somali projects in Somalia. We don't know so much about this community, even though half of our women are cleaning their houses in Italy."

Deeq laughed.

"I know they won't do it," Hanad rolled his eyes, having a moment of déjà vu, as he felt like he had lived this same experience before .

The conversation with Deeq was so fresh that Hanad wanted to meet him again and talk more. Deeq also felt it was important to meet again. A new friendship was born, even though Hanad felt the piercing eyes of Roberto and Kamal for the whole time.

Hanad and the Italian couple had spent a lot of time together for the rest of the five days they were in the country. They flirted with him, touched his body during their many dances, but they didn't do anything to make him uncomfortable. In fact, they protected him whenever others hit on him, as they knew his emotional state was not the best in the world.

It was the best thing to have happened to Hanad because he realized it was the type of friendship he wanted, although he wasn't sure he was into the easy way the couple felt about each other flirting with others. He was still Somali, and he was still very much interested in monogamy, even if his religion allowed four lovers to some.

"I love the way you treat each other," Hanad said one evening, as he shared a meal with them at Mama Roma Restaurant. "You're a real family."

"Yes, we are," Marco said and kissed Luca on the cheek, "I can't imagine what my life would have been like had I not met him."

Hanad sat back and wondered if his Farah would say that about him one day. He wondered if he would turn up and apologize and they too could look forward to a long life of togetherness.

Yes, he wanted that type of love.

CHAPTER 14

For weeks Hanad did not hear from Farah. He had called the hotel Farah was staying so much that everyone was getting sick of him. At first the people did not want to give any information, because of privacy issues for their customers. After calling every day for a week the front desk man finally told Hanad that Farah and his mother had checked out. No, he didn't know where they went. If he called again, the clerk threatened, his name and the telephone number would be forwarded to the authorities.

Hanad became desperate. He found himself suffering from intense emotions from which he had no escape. On the one hand, he was very angry that he had allowed another Somali man to penetrate his heart like that. What was he thinking? It must have been those European films he had watched, gay and straight, which made him weak to certain things. Or perhaps it was those novels he had read in secret. They must have penetrated his psyche, and he hated what they were doing to his thoughts.

On the other hand, he was worried something awful had happened to his Farah. A large part of him knew what he had with Farah was real. Who could have really manufactured such things? Who would ever make love to him like that? Who would ever go as far as to rim him? Who else would let him explode in a tight mouth the way Farah had? Who else would give him the type of experiences he had never known? Who else would challenge the sexual core of his being like that?

It wasn't just the sex for Hanad. It was also the conversations he had had with Farah, both in person and over the telephone, which he felt had enriched his life. Who else would call him on his tribal bullshit? Who else would hold up a mirror to him? Who else would correct his misconceptions and the romantic ideas he has had about Europe and its men? Who else would penetrate his mind with equal passion as his past lovers penetrated his body?

Hanad recalled a conversation he had with his Qur'an teacher years before. The boy had attended a reading of the Hadith at a nearby mosque. According to the Hadith, their prophet had said that marriage accounts for half of one's faith.

"What did he mean by that?" Hanad asked his Qur'an teacher later, as he was afraid to have asked the question during the Hadith reading because the other man was a stranger.

"Marriage brings to us our other half," replied his teacher. "Our spouse brings a part we are missing since birth. Just as we are better off with both of our hands, we are better off with our spouses in life."

Hanad knew that afternoon, as he wiped his tears from his face, that he would want his spouse to be someone like Farah. He realized he wanted someone who would challenge him in all of the areas of his personality and life. Of course, that realization only led to more tears.

For weeks, as Hanad suffered heartbreak unlike he had ever known, Kusow had been pursuing him. When Hanad did not answer his calls, which intensified as time went on, Kusow resorted to parking outside of their home. Hanad ventured out into the world less and less, but whenever he crossed the threshold he would find Kusow. He would be sitting there in his car.

"Please," said Hanad once, "I don't want to talk to anyone." He resisted the tears, "I don't want to meet anyone. I just want to be alone. Leave me alone. Please."

"I'm not expecting anything right now," Kusow replied. "I know you're going through something. I will be here every day until you're ready to tell me what it is."

Hanad was too emotionally worn out to fight with anyone, so he let Kusow be.

Kusow would show up every single day.

Hanad knew very well he was not attracted to Kusow. Kusow was absolutely everything Hanad always said he never wanted in a man. It wasn't just the thick physical body, which he didn't find erotic. It was also because Kusow smoked. Kusow smoked so much that Hanad couldn't remember a moment in which Kusow did not have a cigarette in his hand, in his mouth, or wasn't in the process of lighting one up. He was possessive. He was too crazy. He did not pay attention to the road as he drove. He picked up random men in his car. He was reckless.

Yes, Hanad did not like much about Kusow. However, Hanad could not deny that Kusow was patient. He was principled. He was very funny. He had qualities that Hanad only realized over a long period of time. More importantly, without anything being promised to him, Kusow had been showing up outside Hanad's home for a month. Hanad realized one evening, even though he didn't want to admit it to himself before, that having Kusow out there was a comfort he came to rely on. Day in and day out, Kusow was outside. It made Hanad feel less lonely. It made him miss Farah less. It made him feel things could get better. It made him want to go back to his life.

One evening he walked out of his house and to Kusow's car. Kusow, who did not expect to see Hanad, had sat up and straightened himself.

"Thank you," said Hanad.

"For what?"

"For just being there. I'm not sure why you do it, but thanks."

"I just want to get to know you."

"What do you want right now?"

"Come with me," Kusow smiled.

Hanad got into the car and they drove off.

Kusow took Hanad to all of his favorite spots. Hanad saw everything in the city he had never seen before. They started at Baar Dahab, which had been Kusow's favorite restaurant since childhood, and they ordered his favorite nighttime snack, a halva sandwich.

"*Rooti iyo xalwad*?" smiled Hanad.

"It's amazing isn't it?" Kusow bit into it and took a swig of milk, adding, "I say, the milk makes it perfect."

Hanad realized this was how Kusow had ended up being so chubby. It was this sweet dish. All that sugar in the jelly—not to mention the bread that would turn into sugar later—was simply too much sugar to be consuming at night. At the same time watching Kusow made Hanad all warm inside. There was a child-like contentment on Kusow's face as he had his snack. For Hanad it was like peeking into someone's darkest secrets. He knew Kusow was very much aware of the health effects of eating such a sweet dish in the night, as Kusow had talked about his awareness of health on the drive that first night they had met. But something about the way he was eating it made it worth it.

After that heavy snack Hanad said they should go somewhere to walk. Of course, Kusow knew exactly where to go. Not long after leaving

Baar Dahab they arrived at the Mogadishu Stadium. Kusow knew two of the security guards, as they had grown up together, and he and Hanad were allowed to go inside and to the field. They walked around.

"This is the first time I have ever been inside," confessed Hanad.

"Really?" Kusow asked the question sarcastically. "I'm a little surprised," he giggled.

"Okay, you can stop making fun of me."

"You made it so easy."

Hanad got closer to Kusow and they started holding hands. It felt very natural to Hanad. It was the first time they ever held hands. He realized Kusow's hands were a lot firmer than he had expected. Sure, he was cuddly bear being, but he also had a strong side to him. For some reason Hanad expected Kusow's palms to be doughy. Instead, they felt capable.

They walked around the field for an hour when Hanad said he was getting tired. Then they drove over to the beach and stopped at the Daljiraha Dahsoon. They sat on the steps of the monument. It was now after ten in the evening, the city was a lot calmer, and the breeze was steady.

"Who do you think it was?" Hanad asked, as he looked up on the monument of the Unknown Soldier. The light hit his face perfectly.

"I'm not sure," replied Kusow. His eyes fixated on Hanad's face. Then his eyes too looked up and admired the monument. Kusow could feel the tears sit in his eyes. "He must have been a very brave soldier."

They sat there for a few minutes in silence. Neither of them proposed that, nor was it discussed, but it was mutually felt it was the right thing to be doing. It was as though they telepathically agreed to offer respect to someone who had given up so much for their freedom.

"Want to go to the beach?" Kusow asked.

Hanad wanted to say yes, but he suddenly felt a huge fear come over him. It was one thing to go and hang out with Kusow at his favorite spots, but it was totally another thing to be going to where Hanad and Farah used to make love.

No, he wanted to say no.

No, he thought, Absolutely not!

"Sure," he replied instead.

Hanad didn't want to be stuck on Farah, or the memories he shared with him, and he certainly did not want to make parts of his city off limits to himself just because he had met someone who didn't appreciate their love.

They arrived at Liido Beach about twenty minutes later. As they walked to the beach Hanad began to pull back into his time with Farah. All the memories of the many evenings spent under the moon flooded back to his mind. He could not stop the scenes from playing any more than he could stop his body from reacting. He was stiff, his lung filled with heavy air, his eyes on the verge of flooding tears, and overall feeling very detached from the current scene.

Kusow could see immediately they had made a mistake by coming there. At the same time,

Kusow didn't want to let Hanad know he was aware of what was happening. He didn't want Hanad to feel like he was being jealous or pushy. More importantly, Kusow did not want to spend the evening with someone who was thinking of someone else. So, he decided to get out of this in an elegant way.

"Do you mind if we don't stay here long?" Kusow asked. "I came here with someone in the past," he added, holding onto Hanad's hand firmly. "I want to create different memories with you."

"Okay," replied Hanad.

"Can we go to Jazira Beach instead?"

"That sounds good," said Hanad.

So they drove there. On the way, to take Hanad's mind off the things Kusow played a Dur-Dur song on the cassette tape player. It was a song Hanad had not yet heard. It would be released to the public weeks later. Kusow said it was given to him by a friend of his, who happens to be one of the group's producers.

"You're a very interesting man," smiled Hanad.

Kusow's trick worked. Hanad's mind was shifted. It was no longer on sad memories. Instead, he was actively back in Kusow's world. He was now grooving to a song he wouldn't have heard for weeks had it not been for his handsome new man. Soon Hanad's hand was caressing Kusow's thigh and waving his head back and forth to the beat of the music while the breeze was falling on his face. Kusow would look over and smile. He liked that he had such power over Hanad. Kusow liked that he liked how he made his new man feel. He liked that he was patient enough to be rewarded like this.

It was perfect.

Jazira Beach was too far. Most Mogadishans would only go there on the weekends, and certainly not every weekend. For Kusow it was a new territory, somewhere to make their own memories. Kusow had been the perfect gentleman all evening. Interestingly enough, Hanad was the one who made whatever moves that were made. After walking around the empty beach they decided to sit near the water. It was then that Hanad had reached for a hug.

"Thank you for bringing me here," he told Kusow, as his cheek rubbed against Kusow's. "I didn't realize how much I missed the sea," he added, his hands interlocking with Kusow's. "I'm feeling a kind of joy I had not felt for so very long."

"I'm happy," replied Kusow. He slid his cheeks back so that their eyes were facing each other. "I'm really happy to hear that."

Then, just like that, Hanad placed his lips on Kusow's. They were as soft as they looked. Kusow kissed him back. They kissed and kissed and kissed.

Hanad wanted to kiss him forever.

It was indeed true that Hanad was not originally attracted to Kusow, but soon Hanad found himself more and more wanting to be with him. He would crave his energy, his smile, and that chuckle of his. It was nothing serious, and he definitely didn't think it was going last forever. Kusow was a friend with benefits. At that moment in his life Hanad needed a friend who didn't know his entire history like his other friends. It was impossible to have a balanced conversation with old friends, as the old friends knew his history and would try to compare or contrast with what he was going through.

"No," Hanad would say angrily, "It's not the same as my breakup with Dilifle!"

He would remind his friends that Dilifle was a no-good that he himself had broken up with. This was different. Farah was different. He was an ideal man. He was someone he could talk to. He was someone worldly. He had made the effort to really get to know him. He had touched him deeply. And it finished before it even really started. It was not the same and it was not fair that they were saying it was.

Kusow, on the other hand, listened. He had nothing to judge Hanad against. He accepted Hanad for the person he was presently and not the person he had been while with all those others.

"You're so young," Kusow would smile. "Everything will be fine." Other times Kusow would say, "I'm here in front of you and I'm saying I want you. There are also thousands of men in this city who would want you too!"

Hanad loved the way Kusow reassured him.

"But you know I want more," Kusow would remind Hanad what he felt whenever they would kiss. Hanad didn't feel comfortable doing anything more.

"I know," Hanad would smile.

After weeks and weeks of just kissing it was Hanad who proposed one evening that they do more. They made plans to meet the following evening and they would spend the night together. Kusow called a friend of his who works at a hotel and he booked a room. That night, the two made love for the first time.

Kusow was upgraded from a friend to a lover.

The next day, when Hanad finally returned to his house and neighborhood, he was smiling. His parents were still in Italy and there was no one to scold about his overnight absence. However, that smile turned into a confusion once he learned from the maid that a man named Jamal had been calling nonstop asking for him. Hanad knew what it meant. Jamal was the forger in Bakaaraha market. He had been working on fake papers for him since that ambassador's party. Hanad had jumped at the chance to get an Italian visa. He had been suffering from *bufis*—a psychological ailment that could only be remedied by going abroad.

That was months ago. Things had changed since. He had fallen in love with Farah. He experienced his first real heartbreak. He was now with Kusow. Things had just started getting rosy with Kusow. He was getting more and more attached to the city. It was now full of good memories. He had made his marks. He had visited new areas of the city. He was looking forward to spending more time with Deeq, the young author he had met at that party when the Italian couple was in town.

"But I could be in Rome," he told Roti.

"You're so lucky," sighed Roti.

Hanad had dreamt of living in Rome for so long. He wondered what it would be like to walk around the city of his birth again and see all the beautiful places he had read about. He wondered what it would be like to visit all the landmarks he had seen in those movies.

But what about his chain-smoking, chubby Kusow? He had gotten really close to him now. Hanad hated cigarettes but he loved the way Kusow's mouth smelled because of them. He didn't like chubby men, but he loved the way he felt cuddling up to Kusow's voluptuous body. He loved waking up in the middle of the night and finding himself surrounded by Kusow's big arms while his back rested on Kusow's hairy chest. Hanad felt so safe and protected.

"What should I do?" he asked Roti.

Roti didn't have to think twice about telling his friend to go to Rome. There were millions of men in Italy and he was confident Hanad would find a better match. It didn't matter to Roti that Hanad had all these feelings for Kusow. He wanted his friend to escape from all the heartbreaks these Somali guys were causing him.

"You don't belong here," Roti said to his friend. "I sometimes think you dropped from the sky," he smiled. "I think you will find Rome to be a better place for you in general."

Hanad was left with all these conflicting feelings.

It was nearly morning when he finally made his decision. He would call up Kusow once it was a normal time of day and he would inform him of his decision.

He closed his eyes and tried to sleep.

CHAPTER 15

Making love with Hanad was the most beautiful thing I had experienced in my entire life. All my life everyone said to me, "Kusow, you don't know how to love." Maybe they were right, but now I knew how it feels to make love to someone you love. What made it very special for me was that everything came from him. He was the one who decided to hold hands. He was the one who kissed me and let us kiss into the deep of the night. He was the one who said he wanted to take the next step.

There was one afternoon when I almost gave up. I was sitting in the car, outside of his home, and I was thinking to myself, Why am I letting this boy make me feel this way? Why am I letting him control me like this? I wanted to drive off and never come back.

No, the thought would come, Wait.

I waited. And I waited and I waited, and I'm so glad I did. It has been the most beautiful reward to be loved by him in return. Maybe he doesn't know it yet, maybe he wouldn't admit it to himself, but I know he loves me. It is the way he holds my hands, or the way his lips linger on mine after a kiss, or the way he moans when I throb in and out of him.

So, of course, when he called and said he wanted to meet for lunch, because he has something important to tell me, I knew he had probably came to that understanding.

"So, what's up?" I asked him after we ordered.

Hanad's face turned serious. I knew something was wrong. It was all over his eyes. Hanad hesitated to say what it was.

"I just came from a *mukhalas*," he finally said. My eyes widened at the news. "I met him months ago and he finally got everything together to get me to go to Rome."

I felt like a knife was just jabbed into my heart.

"I'm really sorry," said Hanad, realizing I understood what he was saying. "I have dreamt of returning to Rome for most of my life," he added, tears coming down his face, "I don't want to regret anything."

I wanted to punch him in the face, but I thought, he is just a kid. I didn't make a scene. I was so angry because I felt like he could have saved us both a lot of heartache by telling me all of this before. Then I realized it probably wouldn't have made any difference. I would have still pursued him. Then I got angrier at myself.

"When do you leave?"

"I don't know," replied Hanad, as he wiped the tears off his face. "I think he's got the passport and visa. Now it is just a matter of booking a ticket."

I was confused. "Don't you need to get the ticket before the visa?"

Hanad shook his head. "Of course, it doesn't make sense," he said. "It is the forgery world."

We sat there for a few minutes and neither of us said anything. There was so much I wanted to say, but I didn't want to say anything that I would regret.

"I want to spend as much time as I can with you before I leave." Hanad reached for my hand and looked sweetly into my eyes. "I really—"

"No," I replied, taking my hand back.

"Please."

"No. I already feel like a fool and I don't—"

"Please."

"No."

I didn't even wait for the burger to come. I couldn't be in that restaurant one more minute. I was getting more and more violent inside. I really worried I would do something stupid and I would end up in jail.

I drove straight to Dahir's.

While Kusow had went in search of his friend Dahir's supportive presence, Farah was coming through security at Mogadishu's International Airport. He passed very quickly through Customs because he did not have much stuff. He hailed a taxi.

"Don't you love this city?"

The taxi driver was in a happy mood. Farah, on the other hand, had just survived a long international flight and was not feeling so upbeat about the world, let alone this chaotic city. He returned a small, forced smile at the driver. Of course, that only encouraged the driver more to dive into a larger conversation. Suddenly the man behind the wheel began to tell Farah all about his life. His name was Abdi. He was from Jowhar. He loved the city because he had met and fallen in love with a young woman named Bilan here. She was from a rich family, so he could never really tell her. She had left the city recently and Abdi had dumped into depression.

"However," smiled Abdi into the rearview mirror, "I found love again!"

So soon, thought Farah.

"She fell onto my lap, you could say," laughed Abdi, as he waved through the traffic, continuing, "I was sitting at a coffee shop owned by a relative and it was one of her customers," he giggled, "I'm a lucky man."

Farah thought it was a cute story, and now he too was getting caught up in the romance. He imagined what would have happened if he had ran into Hanad at a coffee shop. Would Hanad talk to him? Would he be forgiven? Would it matter that he came back? Would it be understood that the demons were his and his alone? Would he be lucky enough to have a second chance like Abdi?

"Man, stop that face!" Abdi squinted from the front seat. The car slowly stopped behind another. "I don't allow sorrow in my car."

Farah was startled and smiled.

"Oh, that is much better!" Abdi approved.

Farah liked Abdi.

"Wait a minute," thought Farah, "I think I met you before!"

"Impossible," smiled Abdi, mischievously. "I never forget a face!"

"Do you know Saredo?"

"Oh!" said Abdi, laughing. "You're Barni's son!"

"Exactly!"

"I'm very sorry," said Abdi. "I was very high on love at that time," he added, watching Farah laugh. "Man! What a small world! Here we are I'm picking you up again!"

"Indeed," smiled Farah.

He thought this was a good omen.

CHAPTER 16

The light of the day made its way below the horizon. First, Hanad could see the dim ball of light in the distance, as the sky became colorful. In this painting of nature bright colors were forming. There was a little orange light, as if someone was holding it behind the horizon. Then it crept down and some more until it was fully out of sight. The orange light was now pinkish. The Earth was becoming more and more pink too and the water was glazed with sparkles of pink.

Hanad waited for the sun to fully set. He gazed at the horizon. He could still feel the warmth of the sun in his bones. He closed his eyes to savor the last of the desert warmth.

"Good evening," said a familiar voice.

Hanad didn't have to open his eyes. He knew it was Farah. Part of Hanad wanted to jump on Farah and kiss him all over. Another part, however, wanted to open his eyes and start beating his lover. Instead, Hanad kept his eyes closed.

"I'm so very sorry," Farah said. He stood behind Hanad with his hands embracing the man he loves from the back. "I'm so sorry," he added. He brought his cheek against Hanad's and felt Hanad's warm tears. "I'm a fool, I know that, but I want you to know I'm your—"

Hanad turned around, and his arms embraced Farah. They were now hugging, tight and close.

Dixam cantabo ness morninha … Tristeza di nha vida … Sem consolança dum mãe querida … Sem um doce olhar dum moreninha …

They were playing Cesária Évora in one of the bars in the distance. Her strong voice was carried by the wind and could be heard perfectly over the chaotic waves. Hanad thought it was a good omen to hear one of his favorite singers. Hanad had thought he would never see Farah again, and here he was—hugging him. The musician sang about a black boy who was destined for something great.

Qui sina trista tão profundo … Q'm'ta destinado pa sofrê … Ness nha mundo d'amargura … Nha vida é so dor ma tortura … Antes m'crê more … Pam ca sofrê mas ness mundo …

That night the lovers spent their time at the beach. They talked.

"I want to explain Why I ran away," Farah said. "I was not prepared for love. When I was young, growing up in the cold of England, I was neither here nor there. I was never allowed to be with the foreign children, as my Somali parents worried they would corrupt me."

"That's strange," said Hanad.

"I thought it was strange, too, especially since my family called these people—the white people and everyone else in that country—*ajanabi*, even though we were in fact the foreigners. On the other hand, I spent most of my time with these children in school and in afterschool programs. After my father left the diplomatic world, he worked at two jobs located in two ends of the city. He earned less than what a British person made from just one job. My mother, on the other hand, spent her time chewing *khat* with her housewife friends. So, it was easier to place their children in the afterschool programs paid by the local government. Those programs led to my first sexual experience."

Hanad nodded.

"It was with one of these men who had supervised the children during the afterschool programs," continued Farah, as Hanad listened. "He was a thirty-something man hired as a coach, to oversee the growing talents of their school's soccer team. Aside from getting these boys to perform in their chosen sport, the coach would also talk to us after rehearsals, he would counsel us, and he would just be a figurehead in our lives."

"Okay," said Hanad.

"I was twelve when it happened," Farah said.

Hanad was patiently waiting for Farah to tell the story. He was anxious to hear, but he tried his best not to show it. He held Farah's hand.

"The coach had called my mother and said he would take me out to see a game," said Farah.

Pause.

"It is okay," said Hanad. "You can tell me."

"My mother was happy she didn't have to deal with her difficult son and agreed," said Farah, tear coming down on his cheeks. "Instead of taking me to a game he took me to his home. I didn't have to do anything; the coach did everything. He kissed and sucked me, and he repeated this once a week for months."

Pause.

"I feel so embarrassed to tell you all of this," said Farah.

"Please, don't be. I want to know you."

"Okay," said Farah, squeezing Hanad's hand.

"So, how did it stop?"

"One night, I told him that I would talk to my parents if he didn't stop. Then he stopped taking me to fake games."

Then Farah started to burst into a cry. Hanad hugged him. They hugged for a long time and then when they let go Farah continued.

"I didn't like what the coach did, but I liked the things he did to me. I enjoyed the sexual feelings, even though I didn't like a man who was old enough to be my father."

"I understand," said Hanad.

"It was as conflicting as being told not to spend time with 'foreign' kids when you are spending all of your time with them."

Hanad didn't know how to react to it all. He never dealt with anything like this before. None of his friends experienced these things. He couldn't understand how anyone would be sexually interested in a boy aged twelve.

"I'm so very sorry," he would say to Farah.

Finally, Farah told a third story. "A few years after that experience I was on school break when I met a young Somali at a summer camp. My mother and two of her *ayuto* ladies put together a plan to take their children to the countryside. They rented a house and let all these kids roam in the greenery. It was sixteen children, three mothers, and one male driver in the middle of England."

"Okay," said Hanad.

"The house was amazing," Farah remembered, "I had never been in an English country home before. The first thing I noticed when we drove up to the house was that there was ivy everywhere. It covered so much of what you could see. Then when we went inside the first thing I saw were potted plants. They were on the mantels. They were in the windowsills. They were everywhere."

Hanad nodded.

"I was sharing a room with one of the boys. The boy was 16 and I was 15. We had to share a queen sized bed. The first night we were both tired and fell asleep. The second night, however, things turned sexual once the lights were turned off. The next day we pretended nothing had happened. This continued for two days, but then on the fifth morning we messed around again. Later that afternoon I wanted to talk about what was happening between us. I was developing feelings for the boy, and thought that perhaps we could have some sort of a relationship."

Hanad listened with interest.

"He punched me on the face," remembered Farah, his body actually shaking from the memory.

"Oh, my God," said Hanad. "That is awful!"

"I was so shocked. 'I'm not a faggot!' he yelled at me and stormed off."

"Wow!" Hanad was now really shocked.

"I pretended to be sick and my mother cut the trip short."

"I'm very sorry to hear this," Hanad said.

"So, that is why I ran away."

"What?" Hanad didn't catch it.

"Because of what that boy did, I guess, part of me never trusted love."

"But I didn't do anything like that!"

"I know."

"So?"

"I was still scared."

After hearing all that Hanad said, "I want to know each step. Walk me through why you felt that way."

Farah said, "With you is the first time I have actually fallen in love with someone."

"Really?" Hanad was now smiling.

"Yes, really," Farah squeezed Hanad's hand. "At first it was beautiful and I enjoyed it, but I began to fear my feelings as time went on. My mother's health got better and I used it as an excuse to run away."

"How is she?"

"She is fine. Her health is now very stable, and I was confronted with my feelings. I realized I could not live with myself if I did not really give all to a relationship with you."

Hanad got quiet.

"I want to be with you," Farah told Hanad.

"Well, we have two problems," said Hanad.

"Tell me."

"I am romantically involved with someone else, although it is not serious. I have been thinking of you the entire time. The second issue is that I am about to leave the country. I am planning to go to Rome."

"This 'someone' you met, do you love him?"

"Of course, not," said Hanad.

Then Farah said, "I won't hold it against you that you met people while I was not with you. I understand and accept that. As for going to Europe, can we spend a year together in Mogadishu? We could live together. I'll rent an apartment and you could come and stay as often as you want. We would be a real couple. If, after a year, you still want to go to Rome then we will move together."

"Really? Can you move to Rome so easily?"

"Europe is becoming more and more united," said Farah, "I don't know if you heard but there is something called the Schengen Agreement, which was signed about five years ago. It will eventually mean that all European countries will have open borders," he added. "I could easily make a move to Rome, if that is still your desire."

"And you're not going to run away after a month?"

"I'm back now for good," replied Farah.

Hanad thought for a quick second. Then he smiled and kissed Farah on the lips.

They hugged.

CHAPTER 17

Farah moved into a one bedroom apartment on the third floor of a building on Liido Avenue. Between the kitchen and the living room there was a small area where one could have about a small table and perhaps three or four chairs. The apartment was painted all light blue from the inside, while the outside was painted bright yellow. The best part was a large balcony. One could see the ocean clearly from the balcony. Even though the apartment came with air conditioning, Farah would open the tall Mediterranean door to the balcony to let the place get natural air.

That evening, like every evening since they had rekindled their romance, the boys arrived at the beach at sunset. But now they wouldn't have to stay there too long, they had a place to go back to. About an hour after the sun had set they went to have dinner. Farah took Hanad to a place he discovered when the real estate agent took him out to lunch one day. It was a restaurant owned by Yemeni-Somali family and they served pan-Arabian dishes. Farah recommended that Hanad try a dish called "saltah."

"It's Yemeni," explained Farah, "I had it the other day and it's mind-blowingly good! I think you will like it."

"What is it exactly?"

"Well, it's hard to explain. It is a goat stew with fenugreek froth and something called 'sahawiq,' which is a mixture of many things like tomatoes, herbs, and spices."

Hanad looked at the menu and smiled.

"Try it," encouraged Farah. "You will love it."

"Sure," said Hanad, looking up at Farah, "But what do you think I should eat it with?" Then he looked down at the menu. "I don't think it comes with any—"

"Order some of the flatbread, the 'khubs'."

"And you? What will you have?"

"I want to try the 'makbus,'" he replied.

"You know it's meaty dish, right?"

"Yes," smiled Farah. "I'm not against meat, I just don't want to eat it at every meal, like you Somali people."

"Meat is good for you," smiled Hanad.

"If consumed properly!"

Allah maak ya hawana... ya mfar'ina... Hakm el hawa ya hawana....

Both of the lovebirds enjoyed their food with Fairuz in the background. Hanad was pleasantly surprised he had never heard of the dish he had, although he had known Yemeni people in the past.

After dinner, they walked back to their place. Of course, they had nothing to sit on or sleep on. However, they had a warm place and each other.

"I love it here," said Hanad, as he and Farah stood side by side on the balcony holding hands admiring the view of the sea and beyond.

The lights from houses illuminated the view on one side and the breeze from the sea came from the other. Regardless of what direction they faced they could see only beauty. Much of it had to do with being with the right person. Hanad realized he had never felt like that with anyone. He tried to imagine what he felt with Kusow, Dilifle, or anyone else he had been with—and there were not that many, anyway—and nothing compared to what he felt with Farah.

"It all feels like a blur," murmured Hanad.

"What feel like a blur?"

"The time I spent with others."

"You mean to tell me that the hot time you spent with the hot man you were with while I was crying my eyes out is now, all of a sudden, a blur?"

"Yes," Hanad squeezed his lover's hand. "It is like a fuzzy memory." He turned to Farah and hugged him. "I have never had something like this."

Webiyo isu ooman ... ay wacatameen oo ... waayo badan isdooneen ...

One of the beach hotels was playing Magool. Here was a song about two lovers that found one another, despite all the obstacles placed in their path by the environment.

"I hope you know I was joking with you just now," Farah caressed Hanad's back, "I feel the same way. Nothing I had with anyone before you is meaningful anymore."

"Really?" asked Hanad, as he pulled away from the hug to look at Farah's face in the weak light. He smiled when he saw the honestly in his lover's eyes. He felt a little embarrassed to have asked.

"That is why I came back," said Farah.

"I love you."

Hanad hugged Farah again.

"I love you, too," replied Farah.

They hugged closer.

All was well with the world.

EPILOGUE

Somewhere in the galaxy, the energy of the demon forms—again. The demonic energy heads to Earth and once again zooms in on the globe until the African continent is entirely in its view. Further zooming brings him to Mogadishu. Now he is in the Liido neighborhood and on the balcony of Farah's new apartment.

As the demonic energy forms, so also shows up and forms another energy. The new energy is composed of blinding pieces of light. It is as if a diamond is being shaped. This new energy is building faster than the demonic energy, and it forms into the being of a woman—the same woman Farah's mother had visited, Isnino.

Isnino stands tall outside the door, on the balcony, and waits for the demon to finish forming.

"What are you doing here?" asks the demon, his happy face immediately turning sour.

"I was waiting for you," she replies. "I know why you are here," she adds, as she crosses her arms, not least bit afraid. "I won't let you do it."

The demon peeks through the door, seeing Hanad and Farah making love. "I have been waiting for that boy," says the demon. "He's mine."

"Not anymore," says Isnino, turning to the boys, "I think you know you're too late."

The demon is getting angry, as his face is turning more and more red.

"Go," says Isnino, confidently.

The demon resists. He is squirming. You can see it in his eyes the conflict of wanting what he wants while he knows she is right.

"*Allahu la ilaha ila huwa—*"

"Fine!" he cuts her off. "I'm leaving."

Isnino watches the demon form back to the fire energy, and fly back to the sky. She waits and waits until she can no longer see it on the horizon. Then she turns to the boys.

"Blessed Be," she says, smiling.

She too flies away.

Now really all is well with the world.

ABOUT THE AUTHOR

Afdhere Jama was born in Somalia and grew up in the Mogadishu of the 1980s. When he was a teenager he moved to the United States. He was the editor of *Huriyah*, the first magazine for LGBT Muslims, which was in publication (both in English and Arabic) between 2000 and 2010. His other books include *Being Queer and Somali: LGBT Somalis At Home and Abroad, Illegal Citizens: Queer Lives in the Muslim World,* and *Queer Jihad: LGBT Muslims on Coming Out, Activism, and the Faith.* He lives in New York.

www.ingramcontent.com/pod-product-compliance
Lightning Source LLC
Chambersburg PA
CBHW020655260626
47157CB00008B/3042